SWEETEST REVENGE

. . . don't say a word.

ISBN: 978-0-9880932-2-5
WGA Library of Congress

Edited by Lindsay McDonald
Formatting and Cover Design by I.Designs
Kaila stock © wrangler / Bigstockphoto

www.yvonnemysteries.com

ACKNOWLEDGMENTS

Thanks to Ray and Sheldon for helping with my police research—hopefully I got it right. And of course thanks to all my friends and family for their support.

Chapter 1

"Why are you doing this? Please, let me go. Don't hurt me!" a girl cried as she was dragged out of a black, dirt-encrusted Mustang. She grabbed the door handle and held on for dear life. It wasn't enough though; the man was stronger. Her arm felt like it had ripped out of its socket, making her cry out in despair. Time seemed to stretch for an eternity as they drove from the park to her doom. But now, anxiety rushed through her in an icy flood as a cabin came into view. She knew this was the end and she wanted back into the car.

"Quit fighting," the man demanded. "I don't want to do this. But they're making me!" His last words were filled with a desperation that rung in her ears. Maybe there was hope.

"Please, please. You don't have to listen to them."

Tears ran down her face and she stumbled as he pushed her up the steps. Trying to spin around, she scratched the first thing she came in contact with: his face. She turned and fled, anxiety piercing her chest. With an angry snarl, he followed and grabbed her arm, throwing her towards the weather-beaten door. Looking for something to grab onto, she threw her hands violently towards the man's body leaving another large scratch down his arm, this one deeper than the last.

"Look what you did! Don't move!" He slapped her, knocking her against the door once more.

Before long, she was tied up, sitting in a rickety chair facing a dirty, stained wall, yellowed with age. From what she could see there were very few furnishings. The sparse fittings in sight looked as if they had been dragged out of the garbage. Holes littered the couch and the fabric was worn, with the springs showing through. No curtains were hung; instead, black trash bags were duct taped to the windows. She could just make out the light of the full moon peeking through a hole.

She wrinkled her nose as the smell of rotting garbage wafted towards her, probably coming from the kitchen.

How can someone live like this?

Where is he?

There was a noise from behind and she began to shiver and quake as the footsteps continued advancing.

What did I do to deserve this? Why? Oh God, why?

"I'm sorry, I'm sorry," the man muttered over and over. He began laying garbage bags around her on the floor as he sang, "Hush little baby, don't say a word, Papa's gonna buy you a mockingbird...." He then pulled a large knife from the bag he was carrying. "...if that mockingbird don't sing, Papa's gonna buy you a diamond ring...."

She began whimpering and tried to control the overwhelming urge to vomit. He whipped his head towards her, as if startled she was there.

"Don't start. This isn't my fault. My life was ruined. I can't get it back. Never! Never!"

With the force of a charging ram, he punched her. Blood ran down her lip, mixing with her tears that fell in torrents to her knees. Her ears were ringing and she could no longer discern the mad mumblings of her captor. Losing her equilibrium, fighting back was no longer an option. He had tied her arms behind the chair, and her mind began to go fuzzy as she helplessly watched him duct tape her ankles together. Her world soon became dark.

She woke to excruciating pain and screamed. Flames of agony were buried deep and running along her arm and it took her several mind-numbing seconds to realize that she wasn't on fire. He had his knife buried in her arm and he was digging. She screamed again and barely heard his maniacal laughter. Again and again the knife went deeper into her terrified body.

She didn't know how much more she could take. Her parents' wonderful faces flashed through her mind and the tears continued to track down her aching face and fell onto the plastic garbage bags. She tried to scream, but her voice was hoarse. All of a sudden, he stopped.

Maybe it's over, she thought grimly.

Then she felt his grimy, slippery fingers as they closed around her throat and began to squeeze.

Her body thrashed like a fish out of water. The man could see the life slowly drain from her eyes, then nothing.

He breathed a sigh of relief. It was done. He looked around at the blood splattered everywhere. *Good thing I have the garbage bags.* But blood still moved in a river towards the bags corners onto his floor. He

3

growled a curse; of course, even in death, she was
ruining what little he had left.

He wrapped up her limp body in a few clean
bags and stepped onto the porch. A crunching noise
drew his gaze to the deck and he noticed there was a
pink phone crushed beneath his boot. He dropped the
lifeless body to the ground and picked up the phone,
quickly shoved it in his pocket, and drew a deep breath.
Almost done. He threw her into the trunk of his car,
and then stood uncertainly for a moment, silently
debating if there was time to clean up *her* mess. His
thoughts went back to the blood drying on the floor. He
took his frustrations out on the dead girl in front of him
before slamming the trunk and stomping back to the
cabin. It was good none of the neighbors were around
this time of year, to hear her wonderful screams. The
rich sounds had quenched the fire of vengeance burning
inside of him, for now.

He stripped off his bloody clothes, discarding
them in the garbage bags, and then threw everything
into the fireplace. He grabbed a bucket, a gallon of
bleach, and rags. With a grimace, he knelt down and
fiercely scrubbed the bloodstains, scraping his knuckles
from the force. The water in the bucket had turned
bright red by the time he finished and he could smell
the stench of death in his cabin. He would need to open
the windows before all his possessions were imbued
with the odor. Finally, he was clean enough to dispose
of her. It was too risky having the fireplace burning
while he was gone, so he had everything stuffed
behind the hearth. It would be ready for his return, like
a cleansing, and he could continue with his vengeance.
He locked the door and made sure the windows were
open. The bags were still secure. He then jumped into
the car and sped away, spewing gravel behind him.

He shut off his lights as he drew nearer to the
park and coasted down the gravel road. Hopefully,

from what he had observed, there wouldn't be anyone around the park at this hour. When he popped the trunk open there was a strong metallic smell that made him gag and he covered his nose for a moment.

He could do this; he had to. Heaving the body out, he struggled a moment, almost dropping her. Making no noise was extremely difficult when the bushes were dry and the leaves were brown and crunchy. At least the snow muffled the sound somewhat. He wanted to use a flashlight, but it would stick out like a sore thumb against the darkness. It was good fortune that the full moon shone so brightly from the clear sky and the stars sparkled, casting a faint glow. If he moved slowly, his eyes could adjust enough to keep him away from most of the sharp branches.

This looks like a good spot.

The body dropped to the ground with a quiet thump, and the few leaves left from the autumn season scattered, settling again around the body. If one looked closely, they would have been able to see some blood seeping out of the bags as the encroaching red stained the pure white snow.

"Echo, come back here!"

Shit! Someone's here. He peeked through the deciduous branches, wishing there were more evergreens in the area. A woman came into view with a little dog close beside her and the small dog was trying to veer towards his hiding place. The man felt in his pockets and swore softly. He had forgotten his knife. About to take a step towards them, he froze when the dog was pulled away.

Chapter 2

As Kaila Porter pulled on Echo's leash, she halted beside a park bench, her sides heaving.

A shadow peeled itself away from the trees, pulling farther back into the cover of overgrowth a few steps away.

Hearing a rustle, Kaila glanced around the park before sitting down with a groan. It surprised Kaila how much endurance and speed Echo had, compared to many other Shih Tzus she had seen.

They are such small dogs! Kaila also thought that *with their little legs, they wouldn't move quickly. Wrong!*

Almost at the end of her run, Kaila rested a moment before heading back to her apartment. It was almost nine, so Holly should be home and would hopefully have supper ready. Kaila was glad Holly, her best friend since elementary school, had moved to Calgary with her. Kaila would have been quite lonely without their usual girl talk. Yes, they could have hung out on the phone, but it just wasn't the same as curling up in front of the T.V. and watching a sappy movie, tears streaming down their faces.

Kaila enjoyed the peace and quiet of the park; the path was free of annoying bikers and other runners.

Fall was Kaila's favorite time of year, with the leaves vibrant oranges, hot reds, and shocking yellows. The freak snowstorm that enveloped the city was already melting. She watched as the few remaining leaves lazily falling from the trees spread throughout the park as the wind whistled between the branches. The fallen leaves brought back fond memories of her childhood. She had helped her father rake leaves into a large pile, before running through them, laughing.

The neighborhood she grew up in had trees everywhere. A few of the residents here had destroyed the trees in their yards, making it look like a barren wasteland compared to the others. It was funny watching the older people as they walked by these houses and glared at the empty lots. They seemed to take it personally, even if they lived several houses away.

Watching the scenery unfold helped relieve the stressful day at the police station. It had been a grueling six years, but she had finally made it. Kaila was thrilled with the promotion to detective, even though she was still battling the misconceptions of a few officers. Many thought her father, Chief Grant Porter, had pulled the strings to get her in. She remembered the first few years, the jokes and whispers behind her back, because of her blonde hair and blue eyes. Kaila had heard most of the blonde jokes out there.

What do you call twenty blondes in a freezer? Frosted flakes.

That was just one of many jokes at her expense bantered around the water cooler when they thought she was out of earshot. The jokes had slowly tapered off to only a few diehards over the past years. The others in the department were realizing that she had a great mind for detail and an inner strength that was an asset to any case she investigated. One bright spot was Kaila's new partner, George Hapner. He didn't listen to the talk still floating around and was willing to give her a chance.

Kaila put her hands on her knees and pushed herself up with a sigh. She should really be used to running by now, but every time was a challenge. Kaila would rather be working out in a gym, lifting weights, but her dog Echo needed to get out and walk. Keeping her trim figure was easy. It surprised Kaila that with the amount of garbage she put in her mouth that she hadn't ballooned out. Knowing her luck, it would hit her when she was older and her metabolism stopped working. But until then, Kaila had no real plan to change her ways; she loved food.

Kaila's breath became labored as she turned around the block and her apartment building came into view. She and Holly were fortunate to have found the place; it was only a couple of blocks from Glenmore Athletic Park and Riverdale Park. It was close to both Kaila's police station and the university where Holly was finishing up her medical degree and to the medical examiners' office where Holly worked a couple of hours a week as an assistant. Most of the apartments in the Altadore area were quite pricey, but because of the damage sustained from the previous tenant, theirs had been rented at a discount, for the first few months, anyways.

Kaila was glad to be working Monday to Friday, though of course, that could change depending on the cases. Holly was busy with school and her job, while also fitting in her studying. Kaila was usually in the station by seven in the morning and left around seven. She worked whatever hours George did, Kaila didn't want to be seen as a slacker; she had enough problems. George insisted a couple of times that Kaila wasn't required to come in as early—he was just a workaholic. But she didn't mind. They had the same frame of mind in that regard. Being a workaholic was one of the reasons she couldn't marry her ex-boyfriend. It was also difficult not to spend extra time at the station when they were dealing with a murder case. She could picture the victims' families lining up at the door asking, 'Why? Who was it?'

She was reminded of their last case where an innocent bystander was gunned down during a store robbery. The sixteen-year-old boy's family had come to the station demanding answers. Why was he shot? Was he the target? Who did it? And Kaila could only stand there saying that they weren't sure, but as soon as they knew the family would be the first to know.

That should make anyone want to work harder.

From moving in, unpacking, and settling into their careers, there just hadn't been time for many renovations. The girls had a vision of how the place would look in the end, and with hard work and some elbow grease, Kaila knew they could pull it off eventually.

Kaila pushed the third floor button on the elevator and pulled Echo towards her, before he could begin digging in the garbage can again. He was still a puppy and trying to keep up with his training was difficult because of her work schedule. Echo sat panting quietly, looking around for someone to visit with. She could see the gears in his head turning a mile a minute, debating on how to escape. He was one of the friendliest dogs Kaila knew. Her parents had recommended a nice, large dog for protection, but as soon as she had seen Echo through the pet store window, Kaila was hooked. He was very loyal, and tried discouraging any strangers from coming closer, but he also loved to have fun and played hard.

I should speak to the super, Kaila thought as time stretched. It shouldn't take this long for the elevator to come down. She could just imagine getting stuck in the slow contraption. Most of the other tenants in the building were lawyers and doctors, working long hours as well. She wouldn't be discovered until she was shriveled up, lying in the corner, with Echo gnawing on her leg.

"Hey, Holly, smells good." Kaila closed the apartment door and released Echo, who ran to his water bowl. She looked around their apartment and felt a sense of contentment. She loved the fireplace and enjoyed it immensely in the winter. Even with the multiple holes in the walls and the desperate need for new paint, Kaila was besotted.

"Hi, Kaila, how was the run?"

"Fine, but I'm exhausted. Time for a shower."

The spray felt good. Kaila put her head under the cascading water, and let it wash away the day's dirt and grime. Thinking about the station again, she had known it would be difficult starting there, but it seemed more problems came up than she had expected. The pace was extremely different than back home and at first she had trouble adjusting, especially with the doubt and whispering from the others. But Kaila was strong and wouldn't back down. This was the career she had strived for from the very beginning, and nothing was going to stop her. She could still remember sitting at the kitchen table with her dad, pouring over cases, asking a multitude of questions. The criminal mind fascinated Kaila, leading her down the path of a detective, rather than using her psychology degree. No matter what she expected from a suspect, Kaila was still surprised by the depravity of some. And she had found her kindred spirit in Holly. When a fellow student was murdered during middle school, the girls discovered their mutual passion for solving crimes. As the investigation progressed, they searched, in their own way, for the motive and criminal. Of course, you can't get very far when you're only twelve, but it was the beginning. They had been determined; it was their job to speak for the victims and find the bad guys. Kaila and Holly had never strayed from that path, but continued into their current fields.

By the time Kaila walked into the kitchen, supper was sitting on the table and a pile of books and papers were on the side.

"Thanks a lot, you didn't have to. I can see you have enough today. But I knew there was a reason I wanted you as a roommate!" Kaila said, gesturing to the books and laughing.

"Haha, you're so funny. It's your turn to cook tomorrow, don't forget. I needed a break, anyways."

"Yeah, fine. Maybe I'll just order pizza."

As she was shoving a mouthful of delicious pasta into her mouth, Kaila felt a buzz from her phone. "I have to go," Kaila said, standing up.

"What's wrong?"

"George just texted. A body was found in Riverdale Park. I'll probably be late." Kaila sighed, staring longingly down at her food.

Chapter 3

By the time Kaila arrived at the crime scene, the police barrier was up, the forensic crime unit had on their protective gear, and George was pacing back and forth. He reminded Kaila of her dad; he was tenacious and cared immensely about his cases. An inner strength emanated from him, giving Kaila a feeling of protection, which was good to have in a partner. But George and her father were completely different in appearance. Her dad was tall and distinguished looking, while George was only five-foot-seven with a rather large stomach that peeked out of his too-short shirts...he wouldn't be considered a ladies' man.

"Hi, George," Kaila said, hiking up the slope towards him.

"You're late," George commented before stepping over the barrier.

Kaila grumbled under her breath before following. *I had taken ten minutes, how much faster did he expect?* Pulling on the protective gear handed to her by one of the medics, Kaila walked towards the body.

The murder victim lay partially under a bush, her legs bent at a funny angle, and Kaila could see ligature marks around her ankles. Garbage bags lay bunched beneath the body, stopping the blood from seeping into the snow.

"Do we know who the victim is?" Kaila asked.

"No, there is no identification on her."

"Do they have any idea how long she's been here?"

"Well, rigor is just setting in, so probably not much longer than two hours. The outside temperature isn't cold enough to have much effect. Hopefully with the body wrapped in bags, the snow didn't reach her very quickly. Don't know about the circumstances of her death, though."

They watched as the crime unit continued to map the scene and look for evidence in the immediate vicinity. Kaila pulled out her notebook and began to record the surrounding conditions. *Clear sky, warm, dusk, no wind (died down since earlier this evening), between seven and ten the body was dropped. The leaves lay silently on the snow, looking lost among all the white.*

"I passed this spot about an hour and a half ago," Kaila said quietly.

George looked at her in surprise and asked, "Did you see anything?"

"No, and I'm sure Echo would have noticed her. He was running through the bushes close to the path. I did hear something when I stopped at the bench. I glanced around, but didn't see anything."

"They picked a good time to drop the body, not many people around at this time," George commented. "Hey, clear out, you can't be standing there," George yelled, stomping over to a group of bystanders, waving his arms.

Kaila glanced at the body again and shook her head sadly. A grimace was pulling at the girl's mouth, giving her an angry appearance. *What's her name? Are her parents worried yet?* So many questions

14

needed to be answered. Hopefully some evidence was left on the body so they could find the girl's family. From what Kaila could see, the victim had short brown hair matted with blood and cuts and bruises spread across her face. She was wearing a brown miniskirt, a red shirt and a jean jacket. To Kaila the girl looked to be in her early twenties, but she was terrible with ages.

The girl's body reminded Kaila of when she was living back home in Cremona, she had found the body of Debbie, a close family friend. During the subsequent investigation Kaila's boyfriend had been murdered. The nightmares had slowly faded over the years, and visiting the gravesites became a step in the healing process. Now she tried to at least make it back every year to put flowers on both Justin and Debbie's plots.

"Excuse me."

Kaila jumped out of the way as the body was wheeled out on the gurney towards the waiting ambulance.

"Well, there's nothing else we can do right now, you might as well go home and I'll see you in the morning," George said, as he puffed back up the hill.

Kaila stayed at the scene until the rest of the crime unit was done searching. Darkness had fallen and it was pointless to continue when no one could see anything in front of them. There was a chance evidence could be missed or trampled. A patrol officer would be staying to ensure no one disturbed the crime scene until morning. Slowly walking back to her car, Kaila tried to recall if she had seen anyone or anything on her run, but nothing stood out. A shiver ran down her back as another thought evolved, *I could have run into the killer...and then what?* Glancing around the darkened park, Kaila picked up her pace and reached the car, quickly jumping in. One of the reasons Kaila had joined the force was to bring justice to those who no longer had a voice. It was difficult when they were so

15

young, the girl only looked a few years younger than Kaila. They probably had similar goals, wanting to make some money and have good friends and family to spend it with. Now the girl's family wouldn't ever see that success and probably never got to walk her down the aisle. Kaila assumed she wasn't already married. There hadn't been a ring or any indication of one missing.

The lights were turned off in the apartment when Kaila walked in and she tiptoed to her room, closing the door. Echo lifted his head from his bed in the corner, gave a woof and laid back down. Smiling, Kaila pulled off her clothes and climbed into bed, pulling up the covers. Things were going to work out— she had a good feeling.

The alarm rang at six and Kaila groaned, reaching blindly to slap it off. Taking a few minutes to wake, Kaila waited for Echo to jump on the bed. Their morning ritual was when the alarm went off, he got on the bed and snuggled until she needed to leave for work. Fifteen minutes later, Kaila dragged herself out of bed and hurriedly pulled on her clothes; this wasn't a good morning to be late. George was probably already at the station waiting for the results of the tests, chomping at the bit. However, the test usually took forty-eight hours and she knew the lab was backed up. So it was probably going to be longer. Autopsies, on average, were four hours, so there was a slim chance that the results would be in. Grabbing an apple on her way out of the apartment, Kaila rushed to the station.

I was right, Kaila thought as she strolled into the station. George sat at his desk staring at the computer screen, his fingers drumming on his phone.

"Good morning, George."

George grunted something and continued to stare.

"Have we got anything yet?" Kaila asked.

Without looking up, George replied, "Nothing showed up for fingerprints; she wasn't in the system. I'm waiting for the results of missing persons, but I don't think so."

"That was fast. Why not?"

"She's too recent; there probably isn't a missing person filed yet. You have to wait twenty-four hours before filling out a report."

Kaila sat down at her desk and turned on the computer. More detectives for the morning shift change drifted in and a few glanced at her scornfully before continuing on their way. Kaila just raised her chin and continued to work; she wouldn't let them bring her down. She would prove herself and this case would help.

"So, what do you want to do now?" Kaila asked.

"We'll give it another couple of minutes for the missing person's report and then we'll go and canvass the area and see if anyone recognizes the victim," George answered.

It would be nice if she was in the missing files, then their case could move quickly. They wouldn't waste time trying to discover her identity. Knowing their luck, like George said earlier, the body wasn't decomposed enough for her to be missing long.

"I guess we're doing it the hard way. We'll start canvassing later this morning; it's a little too early for those rich folk" George laughed.

Kaila knew he was probably right, the houses across the park were very large and pricey; most of the homeowners were either from old money and never worked a day in their lives or new money with nine-to-five jobs. They were constantly attending fundraisers late into the evening, they probably wouldn't appreciate an early knock on their door, and

17

persuading any cooperation from them would be difficult.

"Do you have any thoughts on motive?" Kaila asked.

"I'm not sure, there didn't look like there was any sexual assault. Until we find the ID of the victim, I think it will be challenging to determine the motive."

"By looking at her clothes, I don't think she was carrying a lot. No pockets, but she could have had a purse," Kaila said, as George nodded his head in agreement.

At eight-thirty, George grabbed his jacket, motioning Kaila to follow. They trudged out into the cool morning, heading to his truck. They would have to start going door to door and around the park searching for witnesses to the murder.

Maybe Holly would be assisting with the case at the medical examiner's office and Kaila could pump her for some information tonight. If she was working today. The sooner they had evidence, the better. Crawling up into George's truck, Kaila pushed the papers aside before sitting. Someone after her own heart. Holly would hate this; to her, mess was the enemy and whenever possible was cleaned.

"So, how is your wife?" Kaila asked.

"Doing better, the doctor said she could come home tonight. Her heart seems stronger and there isn't any unusual rhythm."

"That's good, hopefully there's no recurrence." Kaila closed her eyes and put her hand on the door for support as George careened out of the parking lot. She regularly feared for her life driving with him and didn't know how long she could survive as his partner. He must have done amazing on the driving test for the police, but she was afraid to ask him in case of offending him and he made her walk.

Fifteen minutes later they pulled up to the park.

"I wonder if we should come back around the same time as the presumed body dump to get the regular runners. Maybe they saw something?" Kaila suggested.

"That's a good idea; we should probably be here around seven. Let's start with the houses."

They started with the homes right across the park. Kaila gazed up at the first one with envy. It was a beautiful home with a large lawn and multiple flower gardens. They walked through the gate, skirted around the large fountain and stepped up to the front door.

A woman answered the door and George asked, "Hello, do you live here?"

"No, I work here," she answered, looking at them suspiciously.

"We're with the police department; can we ask you a question before you get your employer? Were you working last night between six and ten?"

"No, I'm done at six. I will just be a moment." She closed the door, leaving them to wait for about ten minutes before another woman opened the door. She was very pretty with short black hair and stood about five-foot-two.

"Hello, officers, what can I do for you?" she asked.

"Are you the woman of the house?" Kaila asked.

"Yes."

"Did you notice anything unusual last night between six and ten?" George asked.

"I don't think so, what is this concerning?"

"We are just doing a follow up. Did you see a girl in a brown miniskirt and red shirt?" Kaila answered.

"No, sorry I can't be of more help," the woman said, closing the door.

"Well, on to the next," George stated as they left the yard. They moved along the street at a brisk pace, hoping that someone could shed some light. They marked down several houses for a return visit after their canvass in the park tonight. Kaila wished that they were driving in the truck, but it was ridiculous to park at each house along the way. The wind seemed to be blowing right through her thin mitts and her fingers were numb. It was funny how this time of year the weather changed so much, one minute it was beautiful and the next there were snowflakes.

"I'm going to check with the station to see if anyone has filed a missing person's report," George said, pulling out his phone, waving Kaila through the gate in front. This part of an investigation was always tedious and disheartening. It was a lot of talking and cajoling citizens to help the police solve a crime. Kaila was surprised how many people didn't want to be involved. She wasn't sure why people didn't want to help keep their streets safe for their children and family. Right now at their station alone, there were a hundred unsolved cases and many could be closed if citizens would just come forward. Criminals had too much power over regular people and controlled many aspects of their lives, from businesses and even to schools. A lot of citizens thought that the police were supposed to solve the crimes by themselves.

"Well?" Kaila asked on her way back to the curb.

"No one has placed a report yet. Let's finish up this block and then get some lunch. I'm starved," George replied.

He seemed to be a bottomless pit; Kaila was always seeing him put food down the hatch. This could explain his rather large protruding stomach. Growing up, she was used to eating plenty of fruits and vegetables. It was a treat to eat George's regular diet of meat and fries. Her mother never would have let that much fat pass through Kaila's lips.

Chapter 4

"I love Reubens," George said enthusiastically, biting into the large, messy sandwich.

They were at George's favorite lunch spot close to the station. Kaila hadn't seen him go anywhere else and if she made a suggestion it was vetoed. Kaila didn't mind; the food was good, and reasonably priced. With the cost of rent and their other expenses, any amount she could save was a bonus. Of course bringing a lunch would be the best option. Kaila knew if she asked, her parents would help her out, but she was twenty-nine now. Far too old for her parents to be bailing her out.

"So, are we heading back to the houses after?" Kaila asked, shoving a bit of salad into her mouth.

"Yeah, if we don't get any hits maybe a family member will report her missing tomorrow. If I was the killer, I wouldn't dispose of the body in the victim's community, but you never know if you're dealing with a smart criminal." George gave a loud snort. "That's funny; a smart criminal."

Kaila smiled before asking, "Have you gotten a text of when they're doing the autopsy?"

"No, but I think they're a little backlogged, so hopefully tomorrow."

"Well let's get back at it." Kaila dropped some money onto the table and headed for the door with George closely behind.

There was a sense of urgency to find the victim's ID, and then they would have a voice. Right now she was just a Jane Doe with no history. History was very important in solving a crime; it showed how the victim had lived and where they came from. It could also point to possible suspects and motives. They stopped at the station to check in and see if any test results were back yet. Kaila tried to keep the disappointment from rising as they drove back towards the park. It was just the beginning of the investigation; she had to be more patient. She was sure once the newness of her career wore off she would settle in, like George. He seemed like a rock, though maybe a little jaded.

Around suppertime, Kaila and George hobbled up to the last house on the street. They would take a break and then meet in the park to interview some of the pedestrians. Her feet ached and Kaila stopped to stretch out her back as she felt a spasm. It was surprising how fit George was; he didn't seem to be having any difficulties. *I guess looks can be deceiving,* Kaila thought to herself.

"Hello, I'm Detective Hapner and this is Detective Porter, do you have a moment to answer a few questions?" George asked as an older woman answered the door.

"I guess, what's it about?"

"Did you notice anything or anyone unusual last night between six and ten? Also, did you see a young girl in a brown miniskirt and a red shirt in the area?"

"I didn't see anything and do you have a better description of her? That's pretty common."

"She has short brown hair, brown eyes, and curvy. Probably between eighteen and twenty years old." George answered.

"That could be a girl that lives in this area, I think on the street behind us. But I'm not sure."

"Do you happen to know her name?" George asked.

"No, sorry."

"Thanks for your help," Kaila said as the woman closed the door.

"I guess we have a stupid criminal," Kaila commented.

"Do you want me to drop you off at the station or at home?" George asked.

"Home's fine, I can just walk back here after. Are we meeting at seven by the crime scene?"

"Sounds like a plan. I'll see you then." George agreed as Kaila climbed out of the truck and waved goodbye.

Opening a couple of cupboards, Kaila came to the conclusion that pizza was the only option, the right option. Holly walked in just as Kaila hung up the phone.

"Getting supper?" Holly joked.

"Yesss. It's either pizza or starve. I also don't have much time."

"Why, what's going on?"

"George and I have to go back to the park and canvass for potential witnesses."

"Fun. Have you found anything yet?"

"Nada. It's very frustrating. We don't even know who we're looking for." Kaila slouched at the table and stared forlornly at her clenched hands.

"You guys will find something. Don't give up."

"Oh, I won't. I'll get the bastard. Hopefully sooner rather than later. Do you know when the autopsy is getting done?"

"I'm not sure. They're quite a few days behind."

A frown passed across Kaila's face before she could control the reaction. She knew it wasn't the M.E.'s fault, but that didn't make it easier.

The doorbell rang and Kaila hopped up, grabbing her wallet. A young, pimple-faced boy was standing on the other side of the door holding their pizza. He squeaked out the price and held the machine out for Kaila to pay. The aroma caused Kaila's stomach to growl so she hurriedly paid and shut the door.

"That smells good, bring it over," Holly demanded as she smiled.

Kaila was scarfing down her share and Holly gazed at her in wonder. "Are you afraid I'm going to snatch it away from you? I'm sure you have time, so you don't choke." Holly laughed.

"Sorry," Kaila said with her mouthful. "I don't want to miss any potential witnesses."

Kaila ate in record time and made a beeline to the park. She didn't have much time before George would arrive.

Kaila hoped a witness was found. Even when the victim was identified, with no witnesses, it would be difficult to find the murderer.

"George." Kaila waved as she jogged towards him. He was standing close to the crime scene, a smoke hanging out of his mouth and a pensive expression on his face. They decided to each head in opposite directions and question everyone in sight.

There were a few regulars that Kaila recognized from her runs in the park but no one remembered seeing anyone or anything suspicious. Kaila kept track of George's progress as she moved along the path. George was a faint shadow surrounded by the falling dusk. He was moving farther and farther away as the paths diverged.

Kaila made her way to the bench and waited for George to finish. She was now just getting George's leftovers. Huge fluffy snowflakes started to fall, so Kaila wiped the seat before sitting. Pulling off her mitts, she blew into her hands and briskly rubbed them. Soon it would be ski season, something Kaila was looking forward to. Because of the beating Kaila took years ago during her kidnapping, she hadn't skied very often over the last few seasons. Her body had been slow to heal and her spirit even more so. For months Kaila found it difficult to get out and socialize with her friends, and if anyone knew her, they would know that was very unusual. Everything reminded her of Justin. Being a small town, it was almost a guarantee that there would be a special moment in almost every place. He had been taken from her so quickly, with no chance of goodbye. So Kaila was regarding this winter as a new beginning. Her skis were waxed and raring to go.

"Any luck?" Kaila asked as George walked towards her.

"Nope, you?"

"Nothing. Do you want to check those couple of houses we missed before calling it quits? Maybe there will be another resident that can tell us where the victim lived."

"Someone should be home by now. Hopefully it's not too late or they won't be very cooperative."

They trudged towards the first house on the list. The streetlights flickered as they neared and the streets darkened. An ominous feeling came over Kaila as the trees from the park loomed behind them. She could never live right in front of a park knowing what she did about the criminal element. It was different running through. You were in and out and she usually had Echo with her. Kaila would always be looking for someone to jump out. No matter how much training she did, there would always be someone stronger than her. Knowing her luck, that would be who she ran into.

A man answered the door after George rang the bell and glared at them.

"What do you want?" he asked.

George described the girl they were investigating and the man said, "It could be Rachel Walker."

"You know her?" Kaila asked.

"She's best friends with my daughter."

"Can you tell us where she lives?" George questioned, pulling out his writing pad.

"She lives one street back on 15th, number 212."

"Can we have your daughter's name; we may have questions for her?" Kaila asked.

"Victoria. What's this all about?" he demanded.

"We just have a few questions. Thanks, we'll be back," George said as they backed away. The man shut the door as Kaila and George strode away. It wasn't far to the supposed victim's house. Kaila steeled herself; this was the worst part of working homicide. The notification. They stopped in front of the house, partly to stall and partly to admire the beautiful large windows that showed the classy décor within. George opened the gate and stepped through, walking up the stone path to a large wooden door with Kaila trailing behind. There were intricate stained-glass patterns on the door and along the front that weren't noticeable from the street. They seemed to sparkle and glitter, mesmerizing anyone who looked. She wondered what Rachel's parents did for a living. Kaila felt a buzz as her phone received a text and she silently cursed to herself. She had a date tonight with Sam and she was late. There was enough time for her to reply before the door was opened by a rather large woman with her hair pulled back into a severe bun, her uniform impeccable.

"Hello, are Mr. and Mrs. Walker in?" George asked.

"May I ask who's calling?"

"Detectives Hapner and Porter."

Surprise crossed her face as she opened the door further and ushered them into the foyer before disappearing into the adjacent room. Soon an older gentleman entered. He was about six feet tall, black hair slightly balding in the front, with glasses perched at the end of his nose.

"What can I do for you, detectives?"

"Do you have someplace we can talk?" George asked.

"Sure, follow me." Mr. Walker led them into the living room where Mrs. Walker was sitting drinking tea.

"Dear, these detectives want to talk with us."

"What is wrong? Is Rachel alright?" Mrs. Walker cried, setting her cup down.

An hour later Kaila and George left the house. They could hear the sobs of Mrs. Walker as the door slammed behind.

"I don't enjoy those; I'll drop you off at your car because there's nothing more we can do tonight. We'll start fresh in the morning, now that we have a name," George said somberly.

"Thanks."

Kaila looked at her phone and it blinked eight-thirty. *Maybe I'll see if Sam is still interested in getting together,* she thought. Once she texted Sam a message, Kaila hopped into her car and headed home to change clothes. Even though Kaila had had pizza, her stomach still began rumbling. The two pieces she'd been able to gobble down weren't filling enough. *Hopefully Sam won't take too long to respond, or I may give in and eat more pizza, if Holly hasn't taken it all.*

Chapter 5

The apartment was empty when Kaila arrived, except for Echo barking in his kennel. Walking over, Kaila released the latch and steadied herself for his assault. The poor guy, he usually wasn't left in his kennel for that long. He jumped into her lap and tried licking her face while she held him down, laughing.

"OK, Echo, I'm glad to see you, too. I don't have long before Sam should be arriving, if Holly isn't back yet I'll need to put you back in." Kaila swore she saw a pout form on his face as she sat him down. *Speak of the Devil.* Kaila thought as her phone beeped and she saw Sam's text. Great, he'll be here in twenty minutes. Just enough time for her to freshen up. Opening her closet, Kaila peered in, looking for something to wear out to the club. Pulling out one of her favorite red dresses, she grabbed Echo, who had buried himself in the pile of clothes on the floor, before closing the closet doors.

The front door opened and Echo scampered out to greet Holly while Kaila put the final touches on her makeup.

"Kaila, are you busy?" Holly asked, walking into Kaila's room.

"I'm going out with Sam right away."

"Did you find out about your Jane Doe?"

"Yes, her name is Rachel Walker. If you're helping with the case, maybe you could give me a heads up?"

"I'm not sure whose case it will be. Also because I'm part-time they have me jumping around helping everyone."

"OK, I'll talk to you later," Kaila said as her phone buzzed. She bent down, gave Echo a squeeze, and hurried out of the apartment.

Sam was waiting in his Cadillac as Kaila stepped out of the building. They met a couple of months ago at a party and had a few dates. He was a criminal lawyer for a small firm, Bakers & Bakers, and she expected to deal with him on some cases from time to time. Hopefully it didn't cause too many problems, because Kaila enjoyed his company. He loved to rock climb and had gone to many of the same locations as Kaila, and he had a great sense of humor. Sam was someone that Kaila could have fun with and not worry about a relationship at the moment. She was still a little gun shy since Justin.

Climbing into the car, she smiled into his warm brown eyes before leaning over to offer her lips for the kiss she knew was coming. Parting a few moments later, Sam asked, "How was your day?"

"Not great, a woman's body was found in Riverdale Park. But I don't want to talk shop tonight."

"Sure, let's get going; I'm starving."

Walking into the club, Kaila noticed how many eyes followed their movements to the table. Let's clarify: women's eyes. With Sam's deep brown eyes, brown hair, and six-foot-two stature and natural charm, he was hard to resist, so Kaila could understand the attention he drew. She did notice that he never once looked their way, causing her heart to skip a beat. This caused her some concern, but Kaila pushed that aside and decided she would worry about it later.

The evening flew by as they discussed their many different adventures and mishaps. Whenever Sam would bring up anything too personal, like the future, Kaila would quickly steer the conversation in another direction. She couldn't say for sure, but it didn't seem to bother him too much.

They also broke from time to time and joined the overcrowded dance floor as the people gyrated to the songs. By twelve o'clock, Kaila begged off and they headed out to the car.

"Thanks, Sam, that's just what I needed."

"I enjoyed myself too. Maybe we can get together this weekend."

"I'll have to see how this case is going; I'll call you if I have time."

Six a.m. came early and Kaila was ready to continue the search for Rachel's killer. *Just once I would like to beat George to the station,* Kaila thought, putting her purse away and turning to face him. Every morning George was early and looked raring to go, while most other officers required multiple cups of coffee first, herself included. He probably got up at the crack of dawn like her father and sat reading the morning paper.

George sat at his desk flipping through a pile of papers. He gestured for her to take a seat before saying, "We might as well start tracking Rachel's whereabouts the night her body was discovered."

"Do you have any theories on her death yet?" Kaila asked.

"Until we get the medical examiner's report, there are too many unknowns. I'm hoping it's done today. I'll

call Rachel's parents and set up a time to go over."
George picked up the receiver. Kaila glanced at her
watch as her brows drew together. *Seven a.m., not good
timing. But George won't want to hear that from me.*

Kaila logged into her computer and pulled up the
files on their open cases, scrolling through. There were
about forty-five current cases that required their
attention. The department was stretched thin and it
seemed the cases just kept coming in and none were
being closed. It was amazing how many crimes were
committed in just their area of town; she was sure the
caseload was similar at the other police stations.
Working in Calgary was an intense experience
compared to Cremona.

It had been a good start, working in her
hometown, but there was no excitement or mystery.
The biggest event was the murder of Mrs. Wrangler
years ago that Kaila had been caught up in. Otherwise
it was status quo.

Kaila glanced around the station and gave a
little sigh of pleasure. She loved the hustle and bustle
and the fierce pride emanating from everyone when a
cased closed. Even with her rough start, Kaila knew this
was going to be her lifelong career and nothing short of
death was going to take her away.

"Kaila, were you listening to me?" George
demanded, snapping his fingers her way.

"Sorry, what did you say?"

"We're going over to Rachel's in an hour; her
parents won't be ready for us till then."

"They were up? Sure, I'll just investigate them
and then continue looking at these cases."

Kaila searched in their database for Mr. & Mrs.
Walker, but nothing came up, a good sign. Next she
hunted on the web for any information and had
multiple hits for their names. She eventually identified
the correct family and discovered that Mr. Walker was

a plastic surgeon. He had a website that posted testimonials from satisfied customers, many of whom were famous stars. Of course they would never show the unhappy ones. There weren't many details on Mrs. Walker. She was a pharmacist at a local chain in the neighborhood. So the family had money. The Walker family was an old one in Calgary. Mr. Walker's father was a banker and held a great deal of influence in the area.

She still had time after her search, so Kaila put up her feet, leaned back in her chair and read one of the multiple open files from the pile on her desk. When George was assigned her partner, his files were Kaila's first priority. She wanted to familiarize herself with all the open cases and to contribute to the team. But depending on the case, it could take a long time to sift through and learn all the information. There were also times that the information was scarce, only a couple of pages described the crime scene. No leads and not enough time or manpower to continue. Take the case she had in her hands at the moment, George suspected it could be a gang-related shooting, but the victim's ID and the crime scene location were the only information gathered. So far, they didn't have a timeline for the victim or any motive, and to make things more difficult, the victim supposedly didn't have any known family to question. There was a potential witness that swore the victim had associated with a known gang member. It was a mystery and would take a reliable witness, someone to step forward to solve.

It's nice that the police department is finally moving into the twenty-first century and going electronic, Kaila thought as she thumbed through the file. They were starting with the newest and working backwards, putting the cases into the database. Kaila knew that some detectives were having issues sharing their notes and entering them for the world to see, but they would need to get used to it. It was a closely guarded secret who their contacts and snitches were and they didn't want that information accessible. Of course it would help with a lot of the cases. There wouldn't be any issues of ineligible writing or notes gone missing.

"Are we ready to go?" Kaila asked, noticing George grabbing his coat.

"Yeah, I want to get started."

Kaila trailed behind George out of the building, waving to some of the detectives on the way. Compared to the station in Cremona this one was luxurious. Back home the computers were from the Stone Age and the building itself was in need of repair. She knew that her father was trying to coax money from the town, but it was like swimming upstream through rapids...wearisome, with very little accomplished. Some repairs were being done, but it was painfully slow.

Now the station in Calgary was great! They had up-to-date computers and software, the building had been renovated about five years ago, and all their police gear was new. To catch criminals nowadays, the police needed to keep abreast with new technology. Criminals were always trying to stay one step ahead, and it was becoming easier for them to do. There were also many more victims to access, because of the Internet. The police were inundated with fraud calls, most stemming from easy access to the victim's information. Kaila couldn't believe how trusting some individuals were with handing over their personal information online.

Kaila enjoyed the sun's warmth shining through the truck window as George peeled out of the parking lot. She began thinking about Rachel and what had happened to her. The question why could sometimes have a very complex answer and was always difficult to determine. The way Rachel had been dressed, Kaila assumed she was probably going out clubbing or to a party. The parties in that area sometimes got quite a bit out of control with drugs and alcohol thrown into the mix. It seemed that the rich kids had nothing better to do with their parents' money. It may be a harsh way of thinking, but from her experience just in the past couple of years in dealing with these parties, it was a true statement. There were all the frosh parties to deal with as well as the end of summer ones. There had not been any kids that had proved Kaila wrong, yet.

They pulled up in front of Rachel's house and Kaila gazed sadly at the closed curtains all along the front. She had no idea how it would feel to lose an only child, but she could guess. It was a few minutes before the door was opened by the maid. Her bun was messy, her uniform wasn't immaculate anymore and her eyes were red and swollen.

"Hello, we're expected." George said.

"Yes, follow me." The woman closed the door behind them and gestured for them to follow.

Kaila gazed around at the wonderful décor in the entryway. There was a large chandelier hanging and a winding staircase to the second floor. Two large vases sat on the floor beside a beautifully oak-carved desk, which looked quite old. Kaila's feet were cold as they crossed the black and white marble floor. *Who has this kind of house anymore?* Kaila wondered.

When they entered the sitting room, there were four other people along with Mr. and Mrs. Walker milling about the room. Mrs. Walker was sitting in the corner, a handkerchief pressed to her eyes as she gave a short gasp for air. She glanced towards the detectives with bloodshot eyes and motioned for them to sit in front of her. Mr. Walker strode over quickly to stand behind her chair, resting his hands on Mrs. Walker's shoulders and giving Kaila and George a severe look.

35

"Can we make this quick; my wife needs to lie down."

"We'll try, but the first hours of a case are crucial. We need answers." Kaila said, as she scanned the other people pacing back and forth like caged tigers. "Maybe we should talk in private."

"No, they're family and we have nothing to hide," Mr. Walker answered.

"Alright, let's get started then," George said. "We want to establish a timeline for Rachel. When did you see her last?"

"It was Wednesday, so Rachel slept in, she worked the night before. I think she went shopping in the afternoon and was home for supper at four-thirty." Mrs. Walker stopped talking for a moment and wiped her eyes before continuing in a subdued voice, "Rachel was going out with some friends to the club that night; she left at around five o'clock."

"Are you sure about the time?" Kaila asked.

"Yes, we had friends over and that's when they arrived," Mr. Walker answered.

"Why was she going out clubbing so early?" George asked.

"I think she was going to her friend Victoria's first," Mrs. Walker replied.

"Do you know if there was anyone from work or school that was bothering her?" Kaila asked.

"Not that I know of, she never confided in us. She waitressed at the Copper Kettle. Rachel wasn't attending school right now; she was taking a break." The tone from Mr. Walker implied it hadn't been his choice.

Kaila could hear the others moving in the room, but refused to look back. She couldn't tear her gaze away from the parents. Body language told so much more than words. Mr. Walker had tensed up with that last question. Kaila figured with Rachel's parents being such overachievers, her not attending college was probably a sore point. Kaila had been lucky with her parents. Even though she decided to follow in her father's footsteps, they would have supported any endeavor she wanted to explore. Her mother had some difficult moments realizing Kaila was a grown woman, but she was starting to comprehend Kaila's commitment.

The interview continued as the detectives tried to discover a motive for the seemingly senseless murder, but it didn't appear they were going to ascertain it here. Rachel's parents were forthcoming about her life, but tensed whenever their own lives were highlighted. Mr. Walker was a well-known plastic surgeon, especially in his opinion. From what Kaila had seen in the news from time to time, there could be some devastating effects from unqualified plastic surgeons. It didn't seem like Mr. Walker fell into this category.

Before they left, Kaila explained that they needed to go down to the morgue and ID Rachel's body to ensure it was her. There was little doubt, but there were procedures to follow.

"So, what do you think?" Kaila asked George as they left the house.

"I guess we'll talk with Victoria, but unless Rachel had a stalker, I don't see any clear motives. Of course parents are the last to know and are usually in denial where their children are concerned. I know I am when it comes to Pam. I try not to, but it's hard. She complains all the time that she can't pull anything past me; it sure doesn't feel that way," George said ruefully.

They dashed to the truck and Kaila dived in, slamming her door shut just as the wind made a grab for it. Dark clouds were developing above and tree branches waved, briskly flinging their remaining leaves across the windshield. Kaila watched through the glass and grimaced as a few drops fell.

"I hope it doesn't storm, I have a barbeque tonight," Kaila commented.

George just grunted as he glanced past his shoulder and pulled into the street, driving around the block to Victoria's house.

"I wonder if she's home," Kaila said, following George up the walk. She pulled her coat closed as the wind tried to rip it open. Bits of brown leaves and snow swirled around their feet as they walked. It was like watching a dance; a myriad of colors moving over the white contrast of the snow.

George rang the bell as Kaila wandered around the veranda and peeked over the tall white fence looking into the backyard. A variety of vegetation grew as far as the eye could see, with a large pool smack dab in the middle. When she eventually bought her own place that was what Kaila planned to do: lots of trees and shrubs to block out the nosy neighbors. Kaila remembered her house growing up surrounded with plants and trees. Her parents loved gardening and were outside every opportunity they had. Even with all the flowers, Kaila still had room for a swing set and space to run. She was never lonely as an only child. Their neighborhood was full of children and they were constantly at the Porter's house.

They were about to give up when the door opened and a young woman peaked her head out.

"Can I help you?" the girl said, with a heart-wrenching voice, her eyes bloodshot.

"I'm Detective Hapner and this is Detective Porter; we would like to speak with Victoria," George answered, holding out his badge.

"That's me, what do you want?"

"We have a few questions," Kaila said.

Victoria's eyes filled with tears as she answered, "No one else is here."

"That's alright, it won't take long. Can we come in?" George asked.

"I guess," Victoria slowly opened the door and ushered them in. "You can follow me."

As Kaila walked behind, she wondered if Victoria ever ate. She was as skinny as a twig and her blonde hair hung down to her tiny waist in waves. Victoria pushed her glasses back as she motioned to the couch.

"Do you know who did it?" Victoria asked as they sat down.

"No, it usually takes time for us to investigate and find the one responsible," Kaila responded.

"Oh."

"So, how did you know Rachel?" George asked.

As soon as George uttered the words, Kaila watched as Victoria's face crumbled. It was minutes before she composed herself and answered, "We grew up together. We were in the same classes all through high school."

That was just like her friendship with Holly. Kaila couldn't imagine how it would feel to lose her. Holly kept her grounded and held Kaila back from getting into too much trouble.

"So your parents knew each other well?" Kaila asked.

"We all go to the same country club, that's how we met."

"Which club is that?" Kaila asked curiously. She had seen a few around Calgary and sometimes wished she could enter, but then remembering the attitude of some of the rich people she had dealt with, Kaila was thankful not to be included.

"Wyatt's Country Club."

"Mrs. Walker said she thought Rachel was coming over here yesterday before you guys went clubbing, is that true?" George asked.

Victoria's eyes widened and filled with tears as she fidgeted in her seat before answering, "I don't really want to say."

"You need to tell us what you know, Victoria; it might help solve Rachel's murder," Kaila said softly.

"I don't want to get her in trouble," Victoria said, looking away.

"It's too late now; Victoria, please tell us."

"Well, she was going to meet someone. Rachel met him online."

"Do you know his name?" George asked.

"No, she wouldn't tell me. She was very secretive. But Rachel was going to bring him last night to the club to meet us all. She never made it," Victoria said with a sob.

"So you didn't see her at all yesterday?"

"Well, I saw her in the afternoon, we went shopping."

"Did Rachel seem to be in a good mood?" Kaila asked.

"Oh yes, she was very excited. She really liked this guy."

"Did she describe this guy at all; tell you how old he was?" George asked.

"Rachel did say he was older, I think she mentioned twenty-six once. She kept going on about how gorgeous he was, with a great body, and that he played sports."

"What kind of sports?" George inquired.

"Maybe soccer or football. It wasn't a winter sport."

"What time were you supposed to be meeting at the club?" Kaila asked.

"Nine o'clock."

"Do you know where they were meeting?" Kaila asked.

"No."

"Do you know why she would be at the park across the street?" George wondered.

"No!" Victoria looked surprised. "That's where you found her?"

Before either of the detectives could answer, the front door slammed and a male's voice called out, "Victoria, where are you?"

"In here, Dad." Victoria quickly sat straighter and wiped away the few stray tears before plastering a smile on her face.

A large man walked into the room and came to an abrupt halt when he saw the detectives. "I recognize you, what are you doing here?" he demanded.

"We're asking Victoria some questions about her friend Rachel," George answered.

"You can't be asking Victoria questions when she's alone. Her parent has to be here."

"I'm sorry, but she's of age, we can question her. We just want to find Rachel's killer," George replied.

"It's alright, Dad, I want to help." Victoria patted his hand, which was clenched on the back of her chair.

Mr. Bates glared a minute at the detectives before sitting beside Victoria and putting a protective arm around her. Kaila looked quickly down at her notes before she asked, "Mr. Bates, did you see Rachel yesterday?"

"No."

"Did your wife or anyone else in the household see her after the girls went shopping?" George inquired.

"My wife is dead; and no, no one did." Mr. Bates answered in a strained voice.

George and Kaila only had a few more questions before they stood up to leave.

"If you think of anything, Victoria, can you please call us," Kaila asked, holding out her card.

Mr. Bates snatched the card out of Kaila's hand before following them to the door and slamming it behind them.

"Well, that was interesting," Kaila commented as they strode down the sidewalk.

"What was his problem?" George snarled.

"Should we go back to Rachel's and ask to see her computer?" Kaila asked.

"Let's first go back to the station and check if the autopsy is done."

George stepped up to his desk and gave a grunt of satisfaction.

"It's there?" Kaila asked.

"Yep, let's see what the results are. George ripped open the envelope and began reading. Kaila was surprised that the medical examiner's office was still willing to send him a paper copy, but George really didn't like the computer and he had been around the station since the Stone Age. Everyone at the ME's knew him or of him. Kaila watched as a frown developed, and by the end, he didn't look pleased.

"Well?" Kaila asked expectantly.

"Here," George said, shoving the paper towards her. Kaila took it and scanned the contents. Rachel wasn't sexually assaulted, at least that was something. She was stabbed repeatedly, and had bled to death, with post-mortem bruising on her face and upper body. It was a violent death; the killer must have some pent up rage. Was it someone Rachel knew? Did this person want revenge? The girl was only twenty years old, such a short life to have accumulated hate like that. Kaila finished glancing over the report and saw there wasn't any significant evidence left behind by the murderer. DNA was found under her fingernails, but didn't result in a match in the system. Leaves and dirt from the park covered her body with no other foreign material. If they found the knife, the medical examiner could verify if it was the murder weapon, but the police needed a lead first.

"Are there any detectives combing the park where Rachel was found?" Kaila asked.

"Yes, I'm not sure what they've found there. Let's have a chat with the officers, we need something to go on other than this mystery man."

Their arrival at the crime scene halted the activity as the lead detective marched up to them.

"Have you uncovered anything?" George asked.

"No, other than to confirm this was just the dumping ground," the detective answered before turning around and yelling more orders.

"So where was she killed?" Kaila asked. "There wasn't much time to kill her and then drop the body off."

"Maybe in the killer's vehicle. We need to find out who the killer was; I'm sure they couldn't have destroyed all the evidence, they never do," George said as he stared into the trees.

"Let's go get Rachel's computer. There's no point standing here watching them."

"Yeah, fine," George muttered, turning away and stomping to his truck.

Kaila knew how he felt, it was frustrating trying to find a killer and having little or no evidence to go on. Hopefully Rachel's computer could point them in the right direction. If she discovered one boyfriend online, were there more?

Rachel's mom was at home and she led them to the sitting room.

"What do you want? Have you found my baby's killer?" she asked.

Kaila cleared her throat and asked, "Can we get Rachel's computer? We would like to check her emails and correspondence."

"Why, do you think she knew him?"

"It sounds like she may have been seeing someone she met online," George answered.

"That's impossible, she'd have told me."

"Kids don't tell their parents everything," Kaila said gently.

Mrs. Walker frowned at the detectives as she fingered the edge of her blue shawl. Her demure and appearance were completely different compared to this morning. Even though her eyes were red, the puffiness was gone and her hair was styled up in a coiffure with a few strands falling softly on either side of her face. Light makeup gave her a glow that Kaila didn't think she was feeling.

There were no sounds from within the house and Kaila wondered if the guests had left. Perhaps one of them knew about the boyfriend. Or had some insights. Kaila had seen people confide in the most unlikely individuals before.

"Is your husband here?" Kaila asked.

"No, he had to go into work. I'll go and get it…wait here, please." Mrs. Walker slowly rose from the chair and glided across the floor, her heels clicking as she went.

"Why would he go into work?" Kaila questioned.

"I guess it's an emergency to make some woman into a Barbie," George said.

Kaila glanced at him in surprise, but said nothing. She speculated on what they would discover on the hard drive. What kind of sites did Rachel visit? Did she get any threatening messages? Could there be a lot the parents were in the dark about? Rachel was older, but you heard nowadays about the kids in junior high and high school doing drugs so early, even trading sex for drugs they couldn't pay for. *In my day....* Kaila stopped that thought and almost laughed. It made her sound so old and it was a comment her parents made all the time when she was growing up. Even though Kaila was no prude, she couldn't ever have seen herself doing that. The clicking sound of Mrs. Walker's shoes announced her arrival and the two detectives stood up expectantly.

Kaila held out her arms and Mrs. Walker slowly handed over the laptop and said, "There better be no damage to the computer and we want it back."

"It is evidence right now; we'll bring it back when we're done," George answered, moving past her to the front door.

Kaila smiled at Mrs. Walker before following. A light rain was falling as they stepped off the porch so Kaila shoved the laptop into her jacket and ran to the truck, shaking her head in disbelief. *This weather sure was wacky, only here could you find snow one day and rain the next.*

"So, do you think we're going to find anything on here?" Kaila asked. The rain began in earnest and George flung the wipers on high to keep up to the splatters. Hopefully the detectives were done searching the park before the evidence got washed away.

"If she was keeping this guy a secret, there are probably other things as well."

"I hope we find something useful, but not anything extreme for her parent's sake."

When they arrived at the station, Kaila took the laptop to their techs and then headed back to her desk.

"Kaila, wait up."

Kaila spun around and saw Desiree running towards her from the staff room.

"Hi." Kaila smiled.

"What are you doing tonight?" Desiree asked.

Kaila liked Desiree, who had worked in dispatch for the past five years. She was the life of any party and had a get-together every weekend it seemed. Nothing fazed Desiree, men paraded through her life and she was constantly on the move. Being twenty-four, a couple of years younger than Kaila, Desiree made the most of her younger years. Kaila felt ancient compared to her and couldn't understand where all her energy came from.

"I have a barbeque, why?"

"I'm having a few people over, why don't you come by when you're done?"

Kaila smiled before saying, "I'll see how I'm feeling. Is it alright if Holly comes?"

"No problem, I like Holly. See you later." Desiree waved as she left.

For the rest of her shift, Kaila waited on pins and needles for the report from IT while she worked on their other cases. Kaila was finding it difficult dividing her time between more cases. In Cremona, there was usually only one big case going on at once. Here, Kaila felt guilty ignoring one case over another, but time didn't stand still for another case as she investigated. Other leads were going cold and the longer a criminal was loose the harder it was to convict.

Kaila shook out her umbrella as she stepped into her silent apartment. After letting Echo out, she started opening cupboards, searching for ingredients as her stomach growled. She needed a little snack to tide her over until the barbeque, if it still happened. Kaila could hear Echo jumping in the living room as he played catch with his toys. She giggled a little as there was a thump, she assumed he ran into the wall again. He growled for a moment and then he was off. Kaila stared into the dark cupboard and glimpsed a can of raviolis in the back corner. Just as she pulled the can out, the apartment door opened and Holly yelled out, "Kaila, you home?"

"In here." Kaila peeked her head around the corner and waved before going to the stove.

"Do you want some raviolis?" Kaila asked, holding up the can.

"Is that all there is?" Holly grimaced as she leaned down to pat Echo on the head.

"Yep, we really need to go shopping. You can have most of it, I have a barbeque to go to."

"I guess." Holly pulled two bowls out and placed them at the table before sitting down.

"How's work going?" Kaila asked.

"Busy. I can't believe how many murder/death cases there are. And they keep coming. How is Rachel's case going?"

"We're waiting to hear back from IT about her computer. It seems she met someone online and they were supposed to see each other the day of her murder. Of course the parents are the last to know and her mother refused to believe there was someone."

"What about her friends?"

"We have only talked to her best friend Victoria so far. Her work will be next, along with her other close friends. Maybe someone knows about this mystery man, but from what Victoria said, they were going to meet him that night."

"Her parents didn't know about him?"

Kaila snorted. "No. Her dad wasn't home, but Mrs. Walker denied that he existed."

"Do you think it was just a random attack? Maybe this mysterious man?"

"I'm not sure. With the violence it almost seemed personal and there was no sexual assault. I guess it could have been a robbery, but she was going to the club. I don't think she was carrying a whole lot."

"I wonder if she had a stalker from work."

"Well, she worked at the Copper Kettle, not sure how many stalkers she would get there." Kaila carried the pot to the table and dished out the ravioli into the bowls.

"Where's the barbeque?" Holly asked, spooning a mouthful of raviolis.

"Darius is having some friends over, do you want to come?"

"No. Brian and I are going to the movies. But thanks."

"So you and Brian are still going strong?" Kaila teased.

"It's going great, he might be the one," Holly gushed.

"I'm happy for you," Kaila said as she glanced down at the table, releasing a long sigh.

"Are you thinking about Justin?"

"Yes. I know it was over between us, but I miss the closeness. He was a great friend."

The girls were silent for a moment. Kaila thought back over the past years without Justin. It had been a hard adjustment after his murder not to call him up when something happened. He had been there with her for quite a few years; he had been her rock. The trial had been the hardest, not having him there for encouragement while she faced down Giovanni on the stand. She knew that Justin would have said, 'Ignore him, state the facts as you know them and walk away.' Kaila was proud of her testimony; Giovanni couldn't intimidate her, he was going to face justice for killing Justin and trying to kill her.

She needed to go back home to visit Justin's grave. It had been too long. A visit to her parents was also overdue; she expected to see her mom standing on her doorstep any day now.

"Well, I better get ready." Kaila stood up and rinsed her bowl before heading to her room, Echo at her heels. *A bath would feel good, but I'm running out of time*, Kaila thought as she whipped her clothes off and stepped under the steaming water. Afterwards, Kaila played a few minutes with Echo. She could imagine how lonely he got during the day all by himself in his kennel. Sometimes Kaila put his kennel in the living room so he could hear the television. Holly had a good laugh at Kaila's expense, but she didn't mind.

Chapter 6

Darius lived in a townhouse with two friends from college. He was now a struggling reporter looking for a fulltime gig. His goal was to be a journalist and travel to other countries. The rain still drizzled as Kaila stepped up to the house and rang the bell.

"Hello, Kaila, come in." Darius beamed as he opened the door.

"Hey, Darius, how's the grilling going?"

"Without a hitch, weather like this doesn't bother a man like me," Darius said as he puffed out his chest and smiled broadly.

"You're sure you're not going to melt?" Kaila laughed as she handed over her coat.

"Haha, you're so funny."

Kaila followed the noise into the living room as Darius continued on into the kitchen. Four others sprawled throughout the room having a lively conversation, waving their arms in excitement. Kaila felt a buzz as she received a message and she slipped her phone out, reading the text. It was Sam asking for a date tonight. She quickly texted back and then turned to the people in front of her.

There were choruses of hellos as Kaila plopped into the seat and grabbed some chips sitting in the bowl on the glass coffee table in front of her, munching contently. The wonderful smell coming from the kitchen was making Kaila's mouth water and it was all she could do not to shovel the chips into her mouth and awaiting stomach.

Most of the guest were from Cremona and had moved to Calgary after graduation; only John was new to the group. Kaila glanced around the room at the mishmash of furniture. In one corner there was a card table set up with lawn chairs, and in the main area, their flat screen sat on a large brown stand that had seen better days. Kaila was amazed it was still upright. Surrounding the T.V. was a brown leather couch, a green loveseat and a tan rocker. All the pieces were worn, with a patch here and there trying to hold the stuffing in.

"So, Kaila, can I get a quote for the paper about the gruesome murder?" Darius asked, walking into the room, holding up a spoon under his nose.

"No comment." Kaila swiped the spoon away and laughed.

"Well, supper will be ready in fifteen minutes, who wants to help?" Silence followed his question as everyone pretended to look elsewhere.

"You guys are just great! I guess I'm eating everything then." Darius started marching towards the kitchen as everyone jumped up, laughing their protests. Kaila loved meeting with this group of friends, they made her laugh and forget, for a time, the trials of her job.

Kaila grabbed dishes from the cupboard, setting them out on the kitchen table. *At least that was new, so there are no worries of a collapse as we eat,* Kaila thought wryly.

"So, where are your roomies?" Kaila asked.

"They went to catch Ghost Rider 2."

"I saw that movie, it wasn't very good," John commented.

For the next fifteen minutes, they argued about movies and which were the best and worst. With the wide range of tastes, the discussion was quite animated as John and Darius debated the pros and cons of Harrison Ford movies. The words hack, old timer, and great in his time were heard around the table as dishes were passed back and forth. Grilled chicken breasts, shrimp skewers that melted in your mouth, potatoes and salad came her way and Kaila loaded her plate enthusiastically.

"You're going to make some lucky girl a great wife someday," Luke chuckled, spearing another shrimp.

"You can just leave," threatened Darius, as everyone began to snicker.

With their stomachs full, the gang cleaned up the table and migrated into the living room, turning on the T.V. in search of a game. The Stampeders were playing Edmonton, so the egging on began in earnest right away.

"Does anyone want a beer?" Darius called out, his head in the fridge.

A few yeses responded back and Darius entered the room with his arms full. He passed them around and then pushed his way onto the couch before cracking his open and taking a long swallow.

"That is good!" Darius said with a sigh.

By the time Kaila left, everyone was staring at the screen intensely, every now and then letting out a cheer. It was more exciting watching the game now since John was from Edmonton; they had an enemy in camp that they could ridicule. Kaila could feel her body beginning to sag from weariness and decided going to

Desiree's was out of the question. She would probably collapse as soon as she entered her house.

Trying to quietly opening the apartment door, Kaila stepped in just as there was a loud squeak, making her wince. She needed to pick up some WD40 sooner rather than later. Picking her way around the darkened living room, Kaila made her way to her bedroom. No noise came from Holly's room, so hopefully the door hadn't woken her. Echo slept on his bed as Kaila tiptoed past to place her clothes on the chair and grab her nightgown. She then fell into bed and was snoring in minutes.

The alarm woke Kaila from a pleasant dream; she slammed her hand down on the offending noise before she rolled over and pulled the pillow over her head. A rustle sounded in the corner before a bark and a furry object pounced on her stomach, knocking the air out of her.

"Echo, get off!" Kaila said, pushing him away while trying to breathe. Kaila slowly sat up, rubbing the grit from her eyes as Echo jumped off the bed, running back and forth in front of the door.

"I know you want out, but I have to go into the station for a bit." Echo stopped for a moment and growled before resuming his pacing.

"Maybe Holly could take you. I'll be back to take you to obedience training." Kaila moved slowly as she got ready for work. Even though her usual shifts were Monday to Friday, she did work weekends if warranted, but every time it was difficult to have a positive energy on a Saturday morning.

The station was like the morgue. A few detectives were scattered throughout the precinct, but most were out enjoying the weekend.

"Hey, Kaila." George waved as she winded her way to their desks.

"How long have you been here?"

"Just arrived. I'm going through Rachel's case."

"So, what's the plan for today?"

"We need to check with IT about her boyfriend's IP address, if they're in. Also, we need to make a list of her friends and interview them. This mystery boyfriend may be the best lead we have, if we can find him." George continued to scroll through the file as he glared at the screen.

"OK, I'll check with IT," Kaila said.

She strode through the station to the best offices in the joint, the basement. Kaila found it interesting that at all the stations she has been to; the poor IT department had been in the basement, or somewhere similar.

As far as basements go, this wasn't that bad. She walked down a narrow, cement staircase, which spilled out into an open space. Three rooms were joined to the dark abyss, as everyone above called it. *Why, when this building was constructed, didn't they put in plenty of lights?* There was one light hanging in the middle of the room, which cast a looming shadow over the boxes lined up against the walls. Having the computers down here couldn't be good for them. Walking down the steps, she could feel the dampness hanging in the air.

Kaila could hear yelling coming through one of the closed doors as she drew closer. What could be wrong? She quickened her pace when she heard bangs ring out and pushed the door open.

"What's going on here?" Kaila demanded as she gazed around the room. There were desks throughout the room littered with computer components and T.V. screens covered the walls. One lone detective sat in the corner, his back to Kaila, yelling at his screen. Every few seconds, he would bang his fist on the desk. There

55

were ear buds half hanging in his ear and music blared out.

Trying to keep the smirk off her face, Kaila sauntered towards him, making no effort to be silent. She tapped him on the shoulder and jumped back when the detective yelled and pulled out his ear buds.

"Hey, you could have let me know you were there," he snarled.

"I wasn't quiet, you just had your music blaring and you were screaming too loud," Kaila said as she laughed. His face smoothed out and a smile slowly emerged.

"I guess. This computer is very frustrating and, er, I wasn't expecting company today. What are you looking for?"

"I'm hoping you found out where Rachel's boyfriend lives."

"The murder victim from the park? Let me look." He started shuffling through the papers on his desk, slamming his hand on a pile before it toppled over.

"I thought you would be paperless. Why aren't your reports on the computer?" Kaila razed him.

"I know, but I like looking at it on paper. It's easier. Ha!" He held up a paper in triumph.

"Can you email me the information?"

"Sure, I'll do that right away."

"Thanks. I'll let you get back to your music." Kaila chuckled as she walked away.

"You're not funny," he yelled out behind her.

"He's sending me an email," Kaila informed.

"Great! I'm glad someone was there," George replied, not looking up from his papers.

Kaila pulled up her mail and tapped her fingers impatiently until she saw the message come through. "His name is Martin Fernando."

"Where does he live?"

"Can you guess?"

"Right by here."

"Yup."

"Well, let's go pay this Martin a visit," George said with a grin.

"Do you want to grab a bite before we go?" Kaila asked as her stomach growled. "I didn't have time for breakfast."

"Let's eat on the way, I don't want to waste any time."

It was a quick stop at subway and then on to Martin's. Kaila really wanted to try saving money by bringing a lunch, but they were always on the go and she found it difficult. Food never seemed to stay cold in the lunch kits, and weren't very appealing. Of course she was just making excuses; when it came to food Kaila had no will power. And of course George was no help. She remembered when she first started, he had said his wife gave up trying to make him bring a lunch; they were always wasted.

In no time, they pulled up to a modest two-story house. It looked newly painted and well taken care of.

George pounded on the front door and waited impatiently for a response. Soon, footsteps were heard and the door opened. In front of them stood a gorgeous young man, about twenty-five years old. He had short black hair which was mussed and intense dark brown eyes. His clothes were rumpled and he leaned on the doorframe like he needed help standing up.

"Hello, Martin?" George said.

"Yes, who wants to know?" he smiled his pearly whites at them as his gaze landed on Kaila and he gave her the once over.

Kaila could feel a tingle move along her body as his eyes traveled the length of her slim form.

George pulled out his badge and said, "We'd like to ask you a few questions about Rachel."

The smile slid off Martin's face replaced by what Kaila would describe as fear before he slammed the door.

"Kaila, go around back!" George started hammering on the door as Kaila sprinted around the house. *Well, that's surprising,* Kaila thought, bursting into the backyard. She heard him before he came into view, running out of the house towards the alley.

"Stop! Police!"

Kaila took off after him, following as he turned right down the alley. *Hopefully George heard me holler,* Kaila thought as her lungs started to burn. She closed the distance, and before he could step into the street, Kaila tackled him to the ground. She pulled her cuffs out and snapped them on, pushing her knee into his back. *Maybe those runs with Echo are paying off,* Kaila thought with a tired grin. Exercise had not been her plan for the morning.

"OK, Martin, get up." Kaila pulled him none too gently to his feet. He winced as Kaila pushed him in front of her.

"Why did you run?" Kaila needed to stop and rest for a second, but she didn't want to let him go. Just then, George pulled up and jumped out of his truck.

"You caught our runner, did you?" George turned his glare on Martin.

Martin's expression was mutinous as they dragged him to the truck. Kaila patted him down before shoving him inside and climbing in after.

Chapter 7

Kaila and George stared through the glass at their suspect pacing the room.

"Do you think he did it?" Kaila asked.

"I don't know. To me, he's a pretty boy. I don't think he would dirty himself," George answered.

The two detectives marched into the room, slamming the door shut, making Martin jump.

"Why am I here?" Martin demanded.

"Because we have some questions, and you ran," Kaila answered, sitting down and putting a file in front of her.

"Why did you run?" George asked.

"I got scared."

"Why? If you didn't do anything...." Kaila replied.

"I was the last one to see Rachel. I knew you were going to blame me."

"Why don't you tell us your side of the story?" Kaila suggested.

Martin sank into the chair and after several hesitant seconds, began. "I'm not a bad guy. I meet girls on the web, we hook up, and that's that."

"What happened with Rachel?" George demanded.

"We hooked up a couple of times, had fun, but it was time."

Kaila tried to keep the look of disgust off her face, but didn't know if she was succeeding. Martin continued on, "So, I met her one last time that night. To you know...she wasn't bad. But then she started having a hissy fit about breaking up. Said she promised friends we would meet them. And I was like no way; this was supposed to be casual—"

"We get it. What happened next?" George interrupted.

"I was going to drive her home but she got mad and started crying. Rachel demanded I stop and she'd walk."

"Where did you drop her off?" Kaila asked.

"At the park."

"And you didn't follow her home? It was dark," Kaila asked in disbelief.

"She told me to get lost. So I did." By the end of his story, Martin was glaring at the two detectives, his arms crossed over his chest.

"Where did you go after?" George asked.

"I phoned a friend and we went for drinks."

"We need a name and number." Kaila pushed a paper to Martin.

"Fine, but you don't need it. I didn't kill Rachel. I'm a lover, not a killer." He looked impressed with himself.

"Well, forgive us, but we don't believe you and would like an alibi," Kaila snarled. She was reaching the end of her rope with him.

Martin grabbed the paper and wrote down Samantha Parker and her number.

"Really, you met another girl that night?" George asked.

"Of course. The night was still young."

"What time did you drop Rachel off?" Kaila questioned as she imagined her hands closing around his neck and squeezing.

"Around 6:30, I think."

"You wait here," George said before he and Kaila left the room.

As soon as the door closed, Kaila couldn't hold it in. "I can't believe what a scumbag he is."

"I agree, but I don't think he did it."

"I know." Kaila sighed. "He would make such a nice murderer. Do you want to call Samantha?" Kaila asked.

"No, you can. She may talk to a girl more."

"Hopefully she's not there and Martin has to wait awhile." Kaila grinned as she headed to her desk.

The phone rang five times before an answering machine kicked on. Samantha's voice was a high-pitched *squeal. I guess they probably didn't do much talking, knowing Martin,* Kaila thought dryly as she left a quick message.

"I guess we missed her," Kaila told George.

"Ahh, pretty boy's going to have to stay in the hold until we can talk with his alibi." George chuckled as he opened the door.

Martin looked up and watched apprehensively as George approached.

"Stand up," George commanded.

As Martin stood, George pulled his arms behind his back and snapped cuffs on his wrists.

"What's going on? What did Samantha say?"

"She wasn't around, so you'll have to stay the night," Kaila said, following them out the door.

"What! It's still the afternoon. Are these necessary?"

"Yes," George answered, pulling him along. "Don't know if we'll have time to call her later."

"You're not even going to try," Martin accused.

"Of course we are, it would be wrong to leave an innocent in jail," George said blithely as he dragged Martin away.

"That was satisfying," Kaila commented as they walked back to their desks.

"Yeah, but we're back to square one. Who wanted to kill Rachel? Why don't we head out? I'll see you Monday morning and we can go over Rachel's friends," George said, watching Kaila hunched over her desk.

"Sure. I need some rest. We do need to let someone know about the winner," Kaila said.

"Yeah, I'll inform the detective on duty."

Kaila waved goodbye and headed home.

Kaila could hear giggling as she put her key in the door. Her first sight walking into the living room was of Holly laying on the floor and Echo running and barking around her. Every few seconds, he would run in and lick her face.

"Hey, what's going on here?"

"I'm being attacked. Save me!" Holly tried to hold in her laughter as tears streamed down her face.

Kaila dived for Echo's quivering body, but he jumped out of reach and began barking. After chasing and rolling around with Echo, the girls lay exhausted on the couch with Echo between them.

"So, how is the investigation going?"

"Well, we found Rachel's charming online boyfriend. He dropped her off at the park and that's the last he saw of her."

"What! Man, he's an ass!"

"I don't know who we have now. Maybe after a day of rest, we'll have more ideas and luck."

"What are your plans for tonight?" Holly asked as she released the wriggling puppy to the floor.

"First Echo and I have our training, and then I don't know, maybe lay here and watch a movie. My plan is to paint the living room tomorrow."

"Do you mind company tonight? We haven't stayed in for a while."

"Sure, I'd love some. No plans with Brian tonight?"

"No, he has to work."

"OK." Kaila heaved herself up. "I will meet you back here after class. Maybe we can order Chinese food?"

"Great! I'll order the usual for five o'clock."

"Come on, Echo, time to learn your manners," Kaila said, grabbing the wiggling dog and snapping his leash on. He began barking and tried leaping to the ground, tugging on his leash. He knew what was coming and couldn't wait to see his friends. This was their third class and even though Echo was one of the smallest dogs, it didn't stop him from sniffing every dog's butt, enjoying himself immensely. It cracked Kaila up.

They parked in front of a large warehouse and arrived amidst a flurry of activity. A couple of owners ran around the empty room trying to collar their dogs that had gotten loose. Kaila had trouble containing her smile as their barking echoed throughout the building and she felt a tug on the leash as Echo strained to join the activity.

"No, Echo." Echo looked mournfully up at Kaila before he turned back and stared intently at the other dogs.

"Very good," Kaila said, bending down to give him a quick pat. Maybe these classes were beginning to pay off. The rest of the students trailed in just as the instructor strode up with a smile.

"Hello, all. I'm glad to see everyone back. I see a couple of dogs have started off the leash early," he said, gesturing to the two rambunctious dogs. Everyone laughed and yelled out a few greetings. There were a couple of German Shepherds, a Cocker Spaniel, some Terriers, and some that Kaila wasn't sure what breed they were. All she knew was they were vermin dogs, bred to kill rats. She watched each week as the owners tried unsuccessfully, most times, to train them. Of course Shih Tzus weren't a lot better, but there were some gems in the ruff. Even though Echo was a lap dog, his duty to please her wasn't high on his list. But Kaila felt blessed that he seemed more inclined to listen regularly than many others of his breed.

"OK, let's get started. So far we have worked on learning their names and the command to come. We're now going to work on sit."

Kaila smiled in excitement; this is what Echo needed.

"Bring out your treats and if you have a clicker you can use it. We want to lure the dog into position. Place the treat by the dog's nose and slowly raise it so they follow with their head. As they get higher their hindquarters should lower and they'll sit. So, let's try it."

Everyone shuffled through their bags bringing out the treats and the noise increased exponentially as the dogs barked their excitement.

"Make sure you quiet your dogs, we don't want to encourage bad manners."

The noise slowly decreased to an acceptable level, but the dogs continued wagging in anticipation. Kaila held Echo's favourite treat above his nose as his little body quivered in excitement. It was a miracle that he hadn't jumped up and grabbed it yet.

"OK, Echo, let's try this. Follow the treat." Kaila slowly raised it and watched as his attention shifted to the other dogs.

"Come on, Echo, you need to pay attention," Kaila cajoled, getting his attention again. Echo barked and stared at the treat she held.

While owners tried encouraging obedience, some not so successfully, the instructor wandered throughout the room giving advice and support.

Kaila sighed and held up the treat again, saying some words of encouragement to Echo as he stared. There were some triumphant screams as the dogs slowly followed the instructions.

"You can do this, Echo, I know you can." Echo seemed to bark his agreement and focused intently on the treat as it was raised above him. Kaila watched his head lift and held her breath as his butt finally began its decent, and then it happened.

"Great job!" Kaila gushed, giving Echo his treat with a flourish. She grinned as the instructor gave her the thumbs up and continued on.

After about ten minutes the instructor said, "Everyone has had at least one success, so we will try working on 'come here' from last week. Let's line up and we'll try one at a time. We'll try using the sit command and walking a couple of steps away. Grab their toy or treat and if they don't listen, try luring them and rewarding their behavior as they get closer to you. OK, Echo, let's see what you can do."

Kaila used Echo's treat to lure him into sitting and then she walked a few steps away carrying his ball. Kaila glanced back to ensure he was still sitting. The rest of the class watched silently as the instructor stood close to Echo to ensure he stayed in place. He watched her intently and Kaila could see his butt slowly lifting.

"Echo, sit," Kaila said, and he sat back down, making her smile.

She stopped and held out the ball, calling, "Echo, come here, boy." He hesitated for a moment before hopping up and walking to her.

"Great job!" Kaila praised, pulling Echo to her, patting his head and letting him chew a minute on the ball.

"Great job, you two, let's keep going," the instructor said.

The rest of the class flew by. Kaila was proud of Echo; even though it was just a couple of successes, it was still noteworthy. He was excelling at 'come here,' though sitting still needed work.

Kaila practically had to drag Echo out of the building and back to the car after some time off the leash. It was nice that she didn't have to fight him to go to the class. He barked a few more times before hopping into the seat and grinning at Kaila.

"Yes, yes, you did very well," Kaila praised shutting the door.

They walked into the apartment and the delicious aroma of fried rice and veggies excited her nose.

"How did Echo do?" Holly asked.

"Great! You should have seen the dogs this week. They were so cute, and I'm glad it wasn't me trying to lug them around." Kaila let Echo off his leash and shuffled to the bathroom. She pulled off her clothes and showered until the water began to cool, then grabbed a towel, rubbing briskly. Dressed in sweats and a t-shirt, Kaila walked into the living room.

"So, what do you want to watch?" Holly asked.

"Why don't we rent Iron Man 3?"

"Sure, let's get some food." They loaded up their plates, and then headed to the couch for some long needed girl time.

Chapter 8

"I'm going for a walk, be back in a bit." Victoria grabbed her jacket from the closet.

"I don't think you should be going out by yourself."

"I'll be fine, Dad." Victoria leaned over and gave him a quick kiss before leaving the house. Tears threatened to escape and Victoria angrily swiped at her raw, red eyes. The streetlights flickered overhead as dusk began to fall. She needed to get out of the house to breathe; her father was hovering like crazy. It was still unthinkable to her that Rachel was gone and not coming back. Hunching her shoulders against the wind, Victoria continued stepping one foot after another, not noticing her surroundings.

Why would someone want to kill Rachel? Victoria couldn't think of any reason or anyone who'd do such a thing. She fingered the detective's card in her pocket that she had swiped from her father. She had nothing new to report, but not from the lack of trying. Her father wanted her to stay out of it, but how could she? A park bench came into view and she sagged down, staring out into fading light.

A sharp pain on her neck made Victoria gasp and she jerked her hand up.

"Stop!" A harsh whisper in her ear.

Victoria froze and a whimper escaped. "What do you want?"

"I'm sorry, but you have to come with me," the man said as he pulled on her arm and dragged her through the darkened park towards an awaiting car. Victoria tried to struggle, but the knife in her back and the iron grip on her arm impeded her chances. Hope filled her as she saw a man running toward them.

"Don't even think of it, or I'll have to kill him as well," he said and pushed the knife a little harder into her back, bursting through her coat and pricking her skin. Victoria just barely stopped the cry from escaping and pasted a smile on her face as the jogger ran past. He slowed a minute, glancing suspiciously at them, making Victoria's heart beat a mile a minute. She said a prayer before he continued on.

"Good choice." She was pushed against the car, her face mushed into the side. She could hear the door opening. There was a ripping sound and her arms were pulled back and taped together before she was pushed into the back.

"Don't give me any trouble, and we'll see what happens."

Victoria wondered if this was what had happened to Rachel...was Rachel this scared, did she try to escape?

"Who are you? What do you want? Did you kill Rachel?"

"Shut up! I don't want to hear you. You need to be punished."

Tears escaped and ran down Victoria's cheeks, but there was no way she could wipe them away. *What's going to happen to me? Will I ever be found?*

It was quiet throughout the terrifying ride. The man was silent in the front except for his fingers drumming on the steering wheel. Victoria stared out the window at the trees whipping by; they were now traveling outside of Calgary. *Where are we going?*

They lurched to a stop and she slammed into the seat in front of her. Groaning in pain as her nose sunk into the cushion, more tears escaped and trailed down her cheeks. Her car door swung open and the man grabbed her and dragged out by her hair. The doorjamb got in the way of her knee and excruciating pain radiated up her leg.

"Oh my god!" Victoria cried out.

The man just stared at her until there was silence and then began dragging her towards an awaiting cabin.

"Please, please, just let me go and I won't tell anyone."

"Sorry, but that's not possible."

"I didn't do anything!" Victoria wailed.

He was silent while grappling her arm and trying to open the door. *She's just like the other one; whiney,* he thought.

Victoria's glasses fell to the porch and she gave a cry as her vision blurred.

"You won't need those," the man whispered, pushing her in.

The door slammed shut behind them and Victoria could feel the hope drain from her body as she squinted at a chair in the middle of the room surrounded by what looked like plastic bags. What little furniture there was in the room was pushed against the walls, leaving plenty of space. She was dreading the reason why he needed room. Victoria's eye's widened and her body froze with terror, but the man shoved her into the chair and quickly tied her arms and legs. The fight had left her and she only made a feeble attempt to struggle.

"You can't do this! Let me go!" Victoria cried.

"If you don't shut your mouth, I'm going to have to tape it!" he growled. "I'll be back in a minute."

The man grabbed his tools that he would need from the bathroom, where he had scrubbed them clean. Nodding in satisfaction at all the bags on the floor, he slowly walked toward Victoria. He could see the terror in her eyes as he drew closer and she saw the knife. He slowly started to sing, "Hush little baby, don't say a word, Papa's gonna buy you a mockingbird...." He raised the large knife at her and began the slow decent. "...if that mockingbird don't sing, Papa's gonna buy you a diamond ring...."

Victoria began screaming and it didn't seem like it would ever end.

It was music to the man's ears.

Chapter 9

The alarm woke Kaila at eight and she jumped out of bed, excited to start the day. Sleeping in was heavenly. First things first, she needed to take Echo out. Kaila marched to the bathroom. It was nice having it adjoining to her bedroom and not having to worry about wandering the apartment half-naked. She wasn't concerned about Holly, but now and then Brian was a guest; Kaila didn't want to give him a show. Pulling back her hair into a ponytail and quickly brushing her teeth, Kaila headed out of the apartment, Echo at her heels. As they waited for the elevator Kaila snapped on the leash and struggled to keep him from running up and down the hallway in his excitement.

Fog was drifting low in the sky, reaching the tops of the apartments across the street as Kaila stepped out. Their footsteps echoed in the empty streets as they jogged towards the park. Kaila debated on not running by the crime scene, but decided she wasn't going to change her route. But as an afterthought, maybe she should. It's essential to change daily routines, especially if someone was watching. As they ran, Kaila could feel the tension drain from her body and she felt a spurt of energy driving her along. Echo ran happily beside her, his tongue hanging out. He tried once in a while to dart in another direction and was denied.

The wind started to pick up and seemed to blow right through her jogging suit, making her shiver. Once the snow was there to stay, she wasn't sure about running with Echo. He might not like the cold and the truth of it was Kaila didn't want to run in the snow. Some of the runners in the park nodded to Kaila as she ran by and she smiled in return. They came to the fork in the path leading towards the crime scene or east towards the river; Kaila continued east. Her mind wandered back to the crime scene. The tape was removed, reminding people about the murder. Not many knew about the young life that had been snuffed out, and that a murderer was running around free. That was the sad part about working homicide, she lived with a case for weeks and would probably remember it for the rest of her career, while people heard on the news all the time about murders and forgot the next day. The victim was only to be remembered by the family and friends, which was sometimes just a few people. They deserved more than that.

Kaila continued at the fast pace until Echo pulled on his leash, slowing down, his tongue flopping out and his sides heaving.

"Sorry, Echo." Kaila paused a moment to let Echo catch his breath. A man pushed past Kaila wearing blue shorts, a red tank top and matching headband. She shivered just watching him run and rubbed up and down her arms, glad for the black sweater and sweatpants.

"Well, we better get going, it's already seven and I have lots to do today." Echo barked in reply and started to run. They veered around a couple walking with a large lab, causing Kaila to step in an ice-covered mud puddle beside the path. Grumbling and swearing under her breath, she tried to shake her freezing foot out and keep up with Echo. They had managed to avoid the other puddles, but there were too many people now.

Kaila smelled bacon as she and Echo stomped into the apartment, making her mouth salivate and her stomach growl.

"So, what's the special occasion?" Kaila asked, grabbing bacon from the plate as Holly threatened her with a fork.

"I was craving a big breakfast. What are your plans today?"

"I'm going to get painting supplies for the living room. Do you want to help?"

"I can this afternoon, but I have running around to do this morning and I'm meeting Brian for lunch."

"Sounds good." Kaila snatched another piece of bacon before heading to the bathroom for a well-deserved shower. As she lathered soap in her hair, Kaila made a mental note of all the supplies she would need. If she was still in Cremona, she could slip over to her parents' to borrow them, but to drive an hour there and an hour back for that, not likely. She needed mud, trays, paint brushes, paint, drop cloths.... The list went on and on.

Holly was gone by the time Kaila left her room and the only noise was the sound of Echo gnawing on a bone in the kitchen.

"Do you want to go for a ride?"

Echo dropped his bone and began barking excitedly, running around Kaila's feet. She laughed at him while trying to clip his leash on his collar.

The drive was quick to Home Depot and Kaila cruised the lot before finding a spot close to the doors. Ensuring the window was down slightly, Kaila patted

Echo before striding to the doors, excitement coursing through her.

Kaila and Holly had already decided on what color range they wanted, so Kaila pulled out the sample cards, turning them different directions as she stared at them. The plan was to eventually paint the whole apartment, so she wasn't trying to match anything. She wanted a color both her and Holly would like and help them relax and enjoy the space. Finally, a decision made, Kaila lugged a couple of cans and her paint color to the counter and stood in line. Muttering under her breath, she questioned why Home Depot always took forever and there was never anyone to help. But it was the closest store to their place. She sighed as a man bumped into her, trying to step in front.

"Excuse me, sir." Kaila frowned.

"Oh, sorry," he said, stepping away.

To Kaila, it just looked like he was sorry she stood up to him.

Kaila gladly pushed the elevator button and dropped her packages while she waited. It beat lugging them up flights of stairs, even if they only lived on the third floor.

Setting all the supplies by her front door, Kaila grabbed a cookie and mumbled as she spread out the drop cloth and began to tape; she wasn't going to bother pulling off the baseboards.

"OK, Echo, time to go into the room." Kaila picked up the squirming dog and carried him to his bed. "I know, I know, but you'll get in the paint."

Echo growled as the door was closed before he could escape. Kaila grabbed the pail of mud and began filling all the holes.

While she waited for the mud to dry, Kaila grabbed her notebook and pondered Rachel's case. Who could have done this? It wasn't Martin. She started to write down all the possible suspects: stalker, someone from their club, another boyfriend. Kaila stood up and touched the mud, put down her papers and grabbed the sand paper.

"Looking good," Holly said as she walked into the room.

Half the living room was complete and Kaila paused, smiling at her handiwork.

"What do you think of the color?" Kaila asked.

Holly stared a moment at the pale yellow looking back at her. "I like it. Bright and sunny."

"Here." Kaila shoved a roller in Holly's direction. "Get to work."

Holly laughed as she set the roller into the tray so she could take off her coat.

"Alright, slave driver."

The girls worked in companionable silence the rest of the afternoon, finishing the two coats before collapsing on the coach.

"Well, it looks great!" Kaila said with a smile.

"Yup, it was worth the work." Holly agreed, dropping her brush in the tray.

The girls rested a minute before cleaning up their mess and putting the furniture back in place.

For the remainder of the day Kaila worked around the apartment and relaxed, but her mind wasn't far from the case.

Chapter 10

Kaila stretched and glanced over at the clock on her nightstand. She still had fifteen minutes before her alarm rang. There was time to be a little lazy, so Kaila took a long, hot shower, wrapped up in a towel and padded out to the kitchen. Holly found Kaila rummaging in the fridge. "You're early this morning."

"Aah! Man, you scared me."

"Sorry, I didn't think I was that quiet." Holly laughed as Kaila grabbed her falling towel and glared in her direction.

"I actually woke up before the alarm. I couldn't sleep and I figured a good breakfast was in order. I think I'm going to need all my energy. Do you want some eggs?"

"Sure, that would be great. Is it the case?" Holly grabbed the plates and sat.

"I have a bad feeling. I don't think this is over and I'm worried what will happen next."

"I hope your wrong, but you usually have a good instinct."

Kaila grimaced into the frying pan, her mind miles away.

"So, how are you and Sam doing?" Holly asked after a few minutes.

Kaila looked back in surprise before facing the stove and flipping the eggs. "Why?"

"Just curious, I haven't heard you talk about him for a while."

"There's not a lot to say, we're just friends having a good time together."

"And that's it?"

"You know I don't want to get serious right now."

"Are you still holding back because of Justin? That was so long ago."

"No. I do still think about him, and I really need to get out to his grave soon. But I just don't feel that I'm ready for something serious. My career is finally taking off and I'm doing what I love." Kaila started shoveling in her eggs while Holly stared at her a moment.

"Come on, eat up, it's one of the few times I'll cook you breakfast," Kaila urged, waving her fork in Holly's direction.

Holly laughed before following Kaila's lead, dropping the topic for the moment.

"Hey, George, how's it going?" Kaila asked as she shoved her purse into her desk.

"I'm glad to be here."

"What. How come?"

"The wife had a list as long as my arm for me to work on," George grumbled.

Kaila grinned as she grabbed her mug and headed to the coffee station. "Did you get any of it done?"

"Yeah, maybe I'll have to work again next weekend. I'd rather do that than chores."

"What's the plan for today?" Kaila asked.

"We might as well start talking to Rachel's friends and maybe head over to her work later today. Mrs. Walker sent a list over of some of her closer friends."

"Well, hand it over and we can split it."

"Sure."

"So, what happened with Martin?" Kaila asked.

"It's just a shame, but he did have to stay the night." George grinned, "Samantha, that lovely girl, showed up the next morning demanding he be released."

"Really! He sure found a winner."

"Yep. She signed a statement that he was at her place all night, so he couldn't have done it. The detective said she couldn't stop bragging about their time together, he was worried Samantha might start describing what they did. Thank goodness Martin walked in at that moment. She then threw herself at him almost in tears, exclaiming about the injustice of it all."

Kaila snorted. "Sounds like she could be an actress."

Kaila glanced down at the list and saw it consisted of ten friends. She began searching from the top, looking for any information she could. Kaila finished off her second name when George's phone rang.

"Hello," George answered.

Kaila watched as a look of horror passed over his face and he slowly set the phone down.

"What?" Kaila demanded.

"They found another body."

A feeling of dread filled Kaila and she was afraid to ask. "Who is it?" she whispered.

"Victoria."

"Same place." George said gruffly, as he stared out the window.

They trudged through the silent park towards the crime scene. Kaila shoved her hands into her pockets and hunched her shoulders as the wind picked up, whistling through the empty branches.

"Who is doing this?" Kaila whispered as they strode up to the scene.

A swarm of reporters were standing at the bottom of the hill, their cameras pointed at the crime scene.

"How did the vultures find out?" George grumbled.

"Probably listening to the police bands again, and of course, where one goes, the others follow."

"Can you tell us who was murdered?" one of them demanded.

"What happened to them?" another asked.

Microphones were shoved into their faces as they attempted to reach the crime scene.

"No comment!" George growled, pushing them out of their way.

"I can just imagine what they're going to say in the papers tomorrow," Kaila muttered.

George just shook his head and stepped over the tape. Before he could make it any farther, a detective ran over, holding up his hands and yelling.

"You should know better, George; get back unless you're suited up." George spun around and stepped up to Kaila, grumbling under his breath.

"Hey, you knew better." Kaila smiled.

They watched as the team worked, cataloguing and searching for clues. The drop site was a stone's throw away from Rachel's. They really only had one suspect, Rachel's boyfriend, who was definitely looking like a dead end now. *Who else could it be? What was the common link? How many more were going to die?*

80

"Kaila! Are you in there?" Kaila jumped as George shook her shoulder.

"Sorry, I was thinking."

They watched as the gurney was pushed and pulled through the brown, dead grass and snow towards them. *Sort of fitting*, Kaila thought, as she gazed at the gurney and the body beneath the cloth. George put his hand out and lifted up the sheet. Victoria stared back at them with vacant eyes. The only visible signs of murder were the multiple stab wounds on her body; her face was unmarked, other than the frozen terror that Kaila could see. She still had her clothes on, what was not shredded. Something was missing. George started to lower the sheet, but Kaila's hand shot out. "Wait, does something not look right?"

George looked more closely at Victoria before shaking his head. "What are you looking for?"

"I can't put my finger on it," Kaila stated. "Wait! I know! Her glasses. Where are they?"

Kaila and George looked around wildly but they were nowhere to be found.

"Did you find a pair of glasses?" George addressed the detectives in the area. They all shook their heads negatively and continued searching the ground.

"That has to be important," Kaila said.

"Hopefully it will prove who the killer is once we find him; maybe he kept a souvenir."

Kaila stared at the gurney until it was out of sight and then gave a long sigh.

"Let's go try and find a witness," George said, as he stomped to the path. "I'll check with the detectives about who found the body."

"You mean Victoria."

"Yeah," George agreed, quietly walking away.

Kaila pulled out her notebook and stalked over to the nearest jogger, hailing her to stop. She caught the

81

travelling circus out of the corner of her eye and spun around, warning the reporters away.

"Can I ask you a few questions?" Kaila questioned, flashing her badge.

The woman continued to jog on the spot, holding her fingers on her pulse.

"I guess, can you make it quick? I can't stop for long."

"Sure. Have you been in the park long?"

"For about thirty minutes." She glanced at her watch.

"Did you notice anyone strange walking through the park?"

"Not that I saw."

"Did you see a young girl; she was wearing jeans, red high heels and a black jacket?"

"I would have noticed heels, but no."

"Thanks for your time." Kaila watched the girl run away. *That girl must be a diehard runner.* Kaila continued to canvass, but there weren't many people around. She wasn't sure who found the body, but hopefully they had been questioned. There was no one detained for her or George to interview. The reporters stayed just out of Kaila's line of sight, following her along the path. A few times she was tempted to stomp over and tell them what she thought of them, and just barely contained herself.

Kaila plopped down on the bench to wait for George. She could see him in the distance talking with a man and woman who were bundled up.

She could almost feel the heat radiating from them. The woman had a long black coat with a scarf wrapped around her neck and a toque pulled low, covering her ears. The man had a waist length brown coat, which seemed to bulge all around, reminding Kaila of a snowman. *What were they thinking; it was only -15 outside.*

George finished speaking and trailed behind them as they walked towards Kaila. Kaila smiled as they drew near, seeing the man had a large pointed nose, which had turned red-orange from the cold.

"So...?" George asked.

"Nothing. Did someone talk with the witness?"

"Yes, they were questioned and let go. They had a young kid."

"Oh, that's awful. Did the kid see the body?"

"Yes. He's traumatized."

"No doubt. Could the parents give any information?"

"The mom saw a man in the vicinity, but couldn't give any description. She was running after her kid as he ran screaming down the path."

Chapter 11

Kaila knocked on the Bates' door, and waited. The door swung open and Mr. Bates stood in front, a frown on his face. "What do you want? Victoria isn't here right now."

Kaila looked at George in surprise before she answered, "Do you know where she is?"

"Over at a friend's."

"Can we come in and talk?" George asked.

Mr. Bates started to look suspiciously at them, but he conceded and opened the door farther, stepping back. "This way." He led them to the same room the detectives had talked to Victoria in earlier.

Once they were all seated, George cleared his throat, leaned forward and said, "Mr. Bates, we found Victoria this morning."

"What!" Mr. Bates' mouth opened and closed like a fish. Kaila could see his mind working, trying to comprehend George's message.

"Did you arrest her? What did she do?" *He's in denial,* Kaila thought.

"I'm sorry, Mr. Bates, but someone found her body in the park."

"No! That can't be true. My baby!" Mr. Bates put his face in his hands as his shoulders shook.

"Mr. Bates, why didn't you know she was missing? When was the last time you saw her?" Kaila asked quietly.

He looked up with a tortured expression and said, "It was Saturday night. We had a little argument and she went for a walk." He wept as he stared at the detectives.

"So, when did she come back?" George asked.

"She didn't. But that wasn't unusual. We've had arguments before and she goes to her friends to blow off steam. I thought that's where she was. What happened?" Mr. Bates leaned away from the detectives, crossing his arms.

"We're not sure. She was found close to where we found Rachel's body," George answered.

"Was—was she assaulted?"

"They have to perform the autopsy and then we'll know more," Kaila said as she patted his quivering hands. She couldn't imagine how he was feeling. To lose his wife and now his only daughter; he was all alone. Hopefully he had some family and friends close by.

"We're going to need you to come and identify her body," George stated.

"Didn't you do that? How do you know it was her then?" he demanded.

"It has to be a relative. We believe that the victim is Victoria, but a positive identification needs to happen," Kaila said.

"So, there is hope?"

Kaila had to swallow before answering. She didn't want to smash the hope she saw in his face. "It is her, we talked with Victoria for a while."

Mr. Bates' face seemed to wither in front of her. "When?" he whispered.

"The sooner, the better, so we can confirm her identity and continue the investigation."

"Is it the same killer as Rachel's?" he demanded.

"We can't talk about an ongoing investigation. We'll need to regard them as separate cases until we have evidence otherwise. But it is a big coincidence. Mr. Bates, do you have any enemies that you can think of? Anyone that would try to hurt you?" Kaila asked.

"Why would anyone want to hurt my little girl? I can't think of anyone."

"Can you think of someone who knew both girls?" George asked.

"No."

"They have been friends since school. You're sure you haven't met any of their friends?" Kaila said in surprise.

"Victoria never had any friends over other than Rachel. I guess there were a few kids at the club."

Kaila glanced at George before saying, "Do you know their names?"

"There was a boy they were always with. Can't remember his name, though."

Kaila sighed with frustration. "What about activities, are they involved in anything together?"

"No."

"Anyone at the club that you can think of?"

"I can't think anymore. I'd like to be alone now." Mr. Bates stood up and looked expectantly at the detectives. Kaila and George slowly stood and followed him to the door.

"Remember, Mr. Bates, to come by the coroner's tomorrow. Maybe you should bring someone with you for support," Kaila suggested.

"We'll see. You guys just worry about finding the killer." He then shut the door and the foyer lights went out.

"I guess that's a hint he wants us to leave," George said.

"I hope he's going to be alright and not do anything stupid," Kaila said, looking back at the darkened house before walking down the steps to the truck.

"Why do you think Victoria never brought friends home? It's not like it's a horrible place." Kaila gestured behind her.

"Sounds to me like Mr. Bates was a control freak. Maybe she could only bring over friends that were dad-approved, or she didn't want to be embarrassed."

Kaila nodded in agreement as she glanced back at the silent house, imagining the poor sobbing man all alone.

"So, do you want to go check out their club?" George asked.

"Sure, I'd like to see what this club looks like. If they've been going all their lives, there should be lots of members that know the girls."

The first sight that greeted them pulling up to the club was a large golden gate and beautifully landscaped grounds, what was left from the frost and snow. They flashed the guard their badges before he would open the gates, making Kaila feel quite unworthy. A canopy of trees ran along the winding road up to the club which opened into a spacious driveway and a large centerpiece fountain. A bellhop stood at the front doors waiting to move their car, but George pulled up to the fire lane.

"Hey, you can't park there," the valet said in a loud, squeaky voice.

"This says I can," George replied, flashing his badge as he walked by.

Kaila smiled at the kid, but he just gave her a bored look and wandered away.

Kaila was impressed with the room as she entered the main doors, close on George's heels. There was a large crystal chandelier, sparkling like stars, hanging from the ceiling. Right after noticing the chandelier, Kaila's eyes were drawn to a large fireplace taking up a whole wall; it was beautiful. The stone and granite work was amazing.

George marched up to the front desk and rang the bell a couple of times while he glanced around. "I would be afraid to move in here in case I broke something," George muttered.

"Can I help you?" a young man asked.

"Yes, we're from the police department and would like to question your staff and the members here," George replied, showing his badge.

"What's this about?" the pimply-faced kid asked, staring down his nose towards them. Kaila could tell that George was not impressed and hoped he wasn't going to go off on him or they would get nowhere.

"It's about a couple of your members," Kaila answered swiftly.

"Sorry, that's confidential."

"We are investigating a murder, so you are going to cooperate," George stated, glaring at the offending teenager until he looked away and a smug look passed over George's face.

"If you're going to question our members, please be discreet and try to make it fast."

"No problem. Thanks," Kaila said as she dragged George away.

"Who does he think he is?" George grumbled under his breath.

"Come on, who do you want to talk to, the members or the staff?" Kaila asked.

"How about you take the members, the staff are more my style."

"Fine, I'll meet you here when I'm done."

Kaila headed off towards the first room and peeked in; she could feel eyes digging into her back from the kid behind the counter, following her every move. It gave her the heebie-jeebies.

The first room was breathtaking; a piano sat at the far end against a large bay window overlooking the expansive golf course. The walls were cherry oak and stone with a large fireplace and soft seating placed throughout. A few women sat holding colorful filled glasses and a young woman walked quietly among them picking up empty glasses and taking orders. The bar stood in the corner by the piano and a striking man stood behind, wiping down the glasses. The club sure knew how to cater to the women here.

As Kaila walked, she unconsciously smoothed down her shirt and pants. As she neared the ladies, she heard many complaining that the 'help' were slacking, not worth the money they were being paid. Kaila didn't realize that attitude was still around; it reminded her of the dark ages. It was probably a good thing George wasn't questioning the members, because she could picture him wring their necks; he didn't have much patience for the rich and famous, or for idiots.

"Hello, ladies, can I ask you a few questions?"

They all swiveled their heads towards her and just stared suspiciously for a minute.

"Who are you? I haven't seen you around. We are having a discussion here," a woman said, sneering at her.

Kaila took a slow breath. "I'm from the police department and have a few questions about some of your members." She watched as they all glanced at each other before the same woman replied, "I guess."

Kaila pulled out her notepad. "Do you know a Rachel Walker or Victoria Bates?"

"Yes, they both have gone to this club since they were little."

"Do you know if they had any friends here, or anyone that they didn't get along with?"

"They got along with everyone here, they are sweet kids. I can't think of any member that didn't like them. Why all these questions?" the spokeswoman of the group asked.

"Oh," Kaila paused awkwardly. "I'm sorry, didn't you hear that they were murdered?"

All the ladies gasped and they leaned forward with a grin and a light in their eyes.

"When did this happen? What happened; why?" the lady asked.

Aren't these vultures so nice? Kaila thought to herself before answering, "I can't answer any questions about an open investigation. I am searching for potential witnesses."

The ladies started bantering names between them—all of a sudden it sound like there could be plenty of possibilities.

"We can't think of anyone."

Kaila's mouth dropped open. "What were all those names you were mentioning?" Kaila demanded.

"Oh, those were just all the kids that come here. There is one, though, Gerald Radcliff. He was friends with the girls. We saw them together all the time." The other women nodded in agreement and then turned away from Kaila, effectively telling her they were done with this business. She stood in stunned silence for a few seconds before walking slowly towards the bartender.

"I heard you talking to them," he nodded towards the group of harpies. "It's terrible what happened to

Rachel and Victoria. They were lovely girls. My name is Rico," he said, holding out his hand.

Kaila firmly shook his hand before trying to slide hers free and take a seat. Rico hung on a few more seconds, giving her a heart-stopping smile.

I'm sure you look at all the women like that, Kaila thought before answering, "Yes, it is tragic. Did you know them at all?"

"Not well." He had a sly smile as he put the glasses away.

Kaila paused, wondering what he knew. "Did you see who they were with?"

"They seemed friendly with everyone. Every once in a while they would come up to the bar. Of course, that just started recently."

"Did you see them argue with anyone?"

"No."

"Were they real friendly with anyone specific, the ladies mentioned a Gerald."

"Sure, they hung out."

"How long have you worked here?"

"It's been about five years."

"Have you enjoyed it?"

"Of course. It's a great gig, all the members are very generous."

Kaila's eyes trailed to the full tip jar on the counter. She could imagine the tips left by the members, a dream. She'd waitressed for a stint in high school and shivered every time a memory surfaced. The incessant complaining and annoying staff drove her nuts. The customer was not always right, in her opinion. Of course, she didn't leave with much extra in her pocket, it had been a small restaurant.

Kaila asked a few more questions before saying thanks and heading to the next room.

Men were crowded inside smoking their cigars and drinking cognac. Their eyes riveted towards Kaila as soon as she entered, making her feel completely out of place. Plastering on a smile, Kaila began wondering through, trying to communicate with the members of the old boys club. The first cluster of men stared at Kaila and waited until she asked, "I'm here looking for friends of Rachel Walker and Victoria Bates. Did any of you know them?"

"It's too bad about the murders. I talked with Vance. Of course they're devastated," one gentleman replied.

The others looked at him in surprise and Kaila responded, "Both girls were murdered."

The men grumbled and said a few condolences, blaming the young folks of today's society. Kaila just waited until they were done and another man volunteered, "I saw them with everyone at the club, seemed to be pretty friendly girls."

"Did you notice if there's anyone that doesn't agree with your assessment?"

"No."

"I know they hung out with Gerald what's-his-name," another answered.

"You mean Gerald Radcliff?" Kaila asked.

"Yeah, that's the chap."

"What about the staff here, did you see any of them bothering or harassing the girls? Following them around or paying too much attention to them?"

"Of course not. The staff knows their place and they don't loiter around the club members."

Kaila looked at him in disbelief. *Really!* She moved on to the next group before she made a snide comment. No one else could supply any new information about the girls. They were all in agreement about the staff, which annoyed Kaila to no end. Their attitude was from the Stone Age. They really needed to move into the twenty-first century. Of course, with their money, they could afford to have those opinions and no one would argue.

Both Kaila and George were silent as they drove away from the club. Each in their own thoughts, contemplating what they had learned.

Kaila collapsed in her chair and sighed. "That was quite painful. Like pulling teeth."

"Did you find out anything useful?" George asked.

"The girls were friendly with everyone. No one knew of any fights or issues the girls had with any other members. And let's not forget the staff. They know their place and wouldn't dare associate with the members."

"I didn't have much luck either. The staff believes all the guests walk on water. Did you get any names?"

"There was one name, Gerald Radcliff. So, I guess we track down Gerald," Kaila said, looking at her watch.

"How about I write the report for today and you research the club and Gerald," George suggested.

Kaila smiled as she swiveled her chair to face the computer. She knew why George had suggested this; he hated computers. It was enough that the reports had to be written on them, he understood they were a necessity in this day and age, just don't ask him to use them.

Her computer took a minute to load. Maybe Gerald was in the system; it would make things ten times easier. Her fingers flew across the keyboard as she blocked out the surrounding noises. Those typing classes in high school sure came in handy, especially when doing reports. Her parents had insisted on her taking the class. Kaila was still not going to admit to them it had been worthwhile. Gerald wasn't in any of their databases; that was a good sign. Next, she started searching on good old Google. It was surprising what showed up on an individual. Kaila found Gerald's

Facebook page, which he allowed public access. There were a ton of pictures from different parties he had attended. She scrolled slowly through them hoping she could glimpse one or both of the girls. She had just finished the first album when she felt George step up behind her.

"Have you found anything yet?" George asked.

"Nothing. I'm thinking the girls should be in some of these pictures; they were Gerald's friend."

"Stop! Isn't that Rachel?" George asked as he pointed at the screen.

Kaila clicked on the picture to enlarge and studied it for a minute. "You're right, George. She's looking pretty close to that boy she's dancing with."

"Knowing kids today, that's probably normal behavior," George commented. "Back in my day, you sure as heck didn't dance with a girl like that. She had a reputation to maintain."

Kaila laughed. "They still do, but it seems fitting in and being liked is more pressing. Even when I was growing up, I heard talk in school of girls having sex at the age of thirteen. I didn't have time to think about boys at that age. Why ruin my life?"

"Well, let's keep going. Maybe we'll find a few more, and hopefully some will have Victoria."

It took them another hour to finish inspecting all of Gerald's extensive albums. In all, they found fifteen pictures of the girls, all at parties, looking a little inebriated. To Kaila it appeared that most of the kids were drunk and supposedly having a good time. She remembered during her school days going to parties like these and watching the other kids stumbling around; she had never seen the point. Yes Kaila enjoyed having a few drinks, but not to the point where she couldn't walk or talk. Kaila printed off the pictures while George looked up Gerald's number.

"Of course he still lives at home," George said sarcastically. "Kids are being coddled now; they have no sense of self or work ethic. It's the parents' fault for not teaching their children anything worthwhile, and don't let me get started on the school system these days. What the heck are they teaching them; nothing! My daughter's son comes home with this 'new math,' it's ridiculous."

Kaila stared at George with her mouth open as he continued to rant. What had gotten into him? He stopped for a minute as someone answered the phone and he asked for Gerald. A minute later, George slammed the phone down and started grumbling.

"He's not home, and will be out for the rest of the evening. We might as well call it a day. We can talk with him in the morning."

Chapter 12

Holly was standing at the stove when Kaila stumbled into the apartment, dropping her things at the door. Holly glanced over smiling and motioned towards the table.

"You are too good to me. How come you're eating so late?" Kaila asked.

"I just got in."

"How's juggling work and school?" Kaila asked, resting her head on the table.

"Stressful. But I love working at the morgue and don't plan to give it up. I'll just have to live with the hours until I graduate."

"By any chance were you at the office today?"

"I stopped in for a bit, that's why I'm late. How come?"

"Did you see the new body come in? Her name was Victoria."

"Yeah. Why?"

"She was Rachel's best friend," Kaila said quietly, staring at the plate in front of her.

"Really! That's awful. Do you have a suspect yet?" Holly asked, sitting down, a surprised expression on her face.

"No. I can bet you it's the same killer, but we can't assume. We need to investigate it as a new homicide."

"Are there any leads?"

"Not sure about Victoria's case yet, her dad was clueless. We were hoping it was Rachel's new boyfriend Martin, but he had an alibi. I'm not sure where we are now."

"There were no other suspects?" Holly asked in surprise.

"None. Everyone liked Rachel. She wasn't into anything bad, except Martin. He sure was a piece of work; I really wish it had been him." Kaila sighed.

"So, what are you going to do now?"

"We talked to the other members of the club they both went to and found one guy they hung out with, but otherwise nothing. I can't believe that there is no one that doesn't like Rachel. I'm sorry, but nowadays, you can't walk across the street without someone yelling at you."

"That's a little cynical, isn't it?" Holly chided.

"I guess. But no one saw her or is coming forward; it's frustrating."

"Don't worry, you'll get them. You have George on your side and you know what to look for."

"Thanks for supper. I'm going to go soak for a while. Where's Echo?"

"I think he's lying in your room."

Kaila fell face down in her bed with a groan. Her back ached from walking all day. A little snore came from the corner of the room, making her smile. She glanced over and saw Echo lying on his side, his leg twitching every few seconds. It must be a good dream. Kaila dragged her sore body up and headed to the bathroom, the tub calling her name. She ran the water and dumped a couple of capfuls of bubble bath along with Epsom salts into the tub. Kaila hurriedly pulled off her clothes and slowly, inch by inch, lowered her body into the waiting luxury, and sighed with pleasure.

It seemed that no sooner had her head rested on the pillow than Echo jumped onto the bed, licking her face. Kaila grimaced as she wiped the slobber off, pushing him away. She wasn't in the mood for his exuberance. Echo continued growling and pulling on the blanket until Kaila finally gave in and looked blearily at her clock. Crap! It was 7:30 a.m.; she had slept in. Groaning, she slowly swung her legs over the bed and sat up, glaring at Echo as he bounded happily to the bedroom door. "Too cheerful for this time of the morning," Kaila grumbled.

Rushing around the bedroom, Kaila grabbed clothes, threw them on and ran out of the room into silence. Holly must have left for school early; otherwise she would have woken Kaila up.

Kaila's mind ran into overdrive as she grabbed Echo, putting him in his kennel with food and water, before grabbing an apple and running out the door. They would need to talk with Gerald first. Hopefully he could shed some light on the girls. It was surprising that they didn't have anyone else that was close to them. *Only one friend?* She wished Martin's friend hadn't been home yet. Kaila didn't know what it was that bugged her so much about him. Nowadays it seemed like all teenagers/young adults were like him. Maybe it was just the callousness he showed for Rachel's death.

"Hey, George, how's it going?" Kaila asked, rushing to her desk.

George glanced up from his computer screen with a frown. "Fine, I was going to call Gerald soon. I want to catch him before he leaves."

"Good idea. I'll get all the pictures ready."

Twenty minutes later, "Let's go. Gerald's home," George said.

"Where does he live? I didn't have a chance to check yet."

"I'll give you one guess. I wonder if that whole area goes to the same club."

"So, do you think Gerald's going to know anything?" Kaila asked.

"I think the question might be not if he knows, but if he's going to tell us. The way our luck is, it's going to be the latter."

"I really don't understand why someone isn't willing to help out, especially if it's their friend."

"Self-interest. They don't want to get involved, because we might discover something bad they've done. OK, can we go now?" George asked impatiently.

"I'm coming."

Gerald's parents' house was a couple of blocks away from the park, but it was still large and quite beautiful. Kaila rapped the doorknocker and then stood back waiting.

"Hello," Gerald drawled with a wolfish grin. "Who are you?"

Before Kaila could answer, George pushed past and glared at Gerald. "We're from the police department. I called you a few minutes ago."

"Right, right, come in." Gerald ushered them in with a frown.

Not a good sign, Kaila thought to herself as she fiddled with the pictures.

"Have a seat, I don't have much time," Gerald said, flopping in a chair across from them.

"Yes, yes, you have a job," George responded, pulling out his notebook. "This shouldn't take too long."

"You were friends with Rachel and Victoria?" Kaila asked.

"Not really; we went to the same club, but not much otherwise."

"The club staff seemed to think you were friends. You were always seen together," George said.

"I can't help someone else's perceptions."

"All the staffs'?" George demanded. Gerald just shrugged his shoulders and shifted his body, his eyes downcast. Kaila glanced at George before pulling out the pictures and laying them on the table in front of Gerald.

"Can you explain these?" Kaila asked.

Gerald looked up in surprise, "Where did you get these?"

"From your Facebook page."

"I can't help if they show up at the same parties."

"You have an answer for everything," George commented as a smug smile passed over Gerald's face and then disappeared.

"You sure look friendly with them in some of these," George pointed out.

"Fine, I knew them a bit. What does it matter?" Gerald demanded as his body tightened and his fists clenched.

"Why are you lying?" Kaila asked. Her opinion of him had greatly diminished; it was too bad he had just the looks but no brains.

"I don't know."

"Do you want us to take you down to the station? The way we see it, if you're lying, you have something to hide," George threatened.

Gerald stayed silent for a minute, glaring at his hands. Kaila could see the gears turning, determining if defiance was worth it. Would his parents' lawyers be able to help; did he want them to know? When he reached a decision, his body deflated and he seemed to sink more into the chair.

"What do you want?"

"We want to know about the girls. When did you last see them? How often?" George asked, his pen hovering over the paper.

"Why do you keep asking about both girls?"

Kaila was surprised he didn't know yet. "Victoria was murdered as well."

He reared back in shock. "When?" he demanded.

"Yesterday," George answered.

Gerald put his face into his hands and stayed motionless for a few minutes, his shoulders visibly shaking.

"Well?" Gerald asked.

"When was the last time you saw either girl?" Kaila asked.

"On the weekend, we were at Delia's party."

"Who's she?"

"A girl we went to school with."

"Does she live in this area?"

"No, farther south."

"Is she a member at your club? Do you associate much other than the party?"

"She's more a party friend; her family doesn't associate with our club. I don't think they joined anywhere."

"Can you give me her contact information?" Kaila asked, handing over her notebook and pen. Gerald reached over slowly and wrote down Delia's name and number.

"Was there anyone you didn't recognize at the party?" George asked.

"I don't know, it was a big party. I don't think so." Gerald frowned.

"What about the girls, did you see anyone harassing them?"

"Both Victoria and Rachel are pretty friendly, if you know what I mean. I don't think there was anyone that didn't like them." He grinned.

"Do you mean they slept around a lot?" Kaila asked.

"No, but they sure liked to fool around."

"Did you fool around with them?"

It took Gerald a minute to reply, "With Rachel when we were in school, but it didn't go far. Not Victoria, though." He shook his head.

"What was wrong with Victoria?" Kaila demanded, trying not to be insulted for her.

"It was more like brother and sister with her."

"Well, was there someone you knew that was upset they didn't get farther than second base?" George asked.

"I didn't hear, and you know how guys will talk."

"If you think of anyone, please call," Kaila said, handing over her card.

Kaila and George were sitting in the truck when Gerald squealed out of the garage.

"Punk," George mumbled.

"We seem to keep hitting brick walls." Kaila sighed. "This case is evolving and leaving us behind. I'm afraid to ask what's going to happen next."

"We'll catch the bastard; it's just a matter of time. He'll slip up. They always do."

"Hopefully, it's in enough time. Well, we have this Delia to call. Maybe she noticed someone since it was her party. But I know how parties get out of control, guests bringing everyone they know."

George pulled away from the house and headed back to the station.

"Have we gotten the autopsy for Victoria?" Kaila asked, as they reached their desks.

"They were supposed to send it over this morning. I hope it's here," George answered, rifling through his papers. A smile crossed his face. "They must be rushing things through, because here it is." George pulled out the file triumphantly.

"I think the higher-ups know the cases are connected and don't want a serial killer on their hands. If the media ever caught on, they would drive the public into a frenzy. Of course, we know it's a forgone conclusion that the media will sniff it out. It's just a matter of time before this is out. This morning I saw an article about Victoria's murder in the paper, but no connection yet." He sighed and rubbed his eyes. "Victoria has the same wounds as Rachel, looks like the same weapon. But until we find the murder weapon to compare, we won't know for sure." George glanced up.

"That is good news, validates what we have been saying. Any sexual assault?"

"No. They found a hair, and it matched the DNA from Rachel's case," George said, frowning.

"Why are these girls being targeted? They're pretty and young, but no sexual assault. The attack is violent, so you would think the suspect is angry about something. Maybe a grudge against women? Was he abused? We still don't have a motive for it to be personal against the victims. Our suspect pool is extremely low, nonexistent, actually. Who are we going to talk to now?"

"We need to finish with Rachel and Victoria's friends and now we have the party to look at. Then figure out whom and what they have in common. Maybe also relook at the Country Club. With all that money, there's bound to be someone unhappy. Maybe enough for a motive."

"I can look at the family and friends angle. I'm wondering if something happened at the party that weekend. The girls could have picked up a stalker, with all the booze and drugs; someone might have been pissed by a rejection."

"Sure, I'll check into the club's background."

Kaila picked up the phone and dialed Delia's number. After the third ring, a girl answered.

"Can I speak with Delia?"

"Speaking." *Man does she sound old*, Kaila thought.

"I'm Detective Porter, are you available for me to swing by? I have some questions about Rachel Walker and Victoria Bates."

"Why?"

"We are investigating Rachel Walker and Victoria Bates's murders. Gerald Radcliff said the girls were at your party."

"I guess."

"I will be over in twenty. Thanks."

Kaila dropped the phone and grabbed her purse. "I'm off to talk with Delia."

"Good luck," George replied not looking up from his papers.

It was exactly twenty minutes later when Kaila pulled up in front of Delia's parents' house. George's comments came back to her about spoiled kids not leaving home, making her smile in agreement. Kaila couldn't help but compare Delia's house with the victims and it surprisingly fell short. The home was a modest two-story dwelling in an older neighbourhood. The yard was well cared for and the house's light yellow siding shone as the sun glittered off it. Before Kaila made it up the steps, the door swung open and Kaila assumed Delia stood in front of her. She was stunning. Her black hair was cut in a cute bob framing her thin face, and she had full lips that every girl probably envied. Her body was the perfect hourglass figure, with no fat in sight. To Kaila, Delia looked closer to her age.

"Hello, I'm Detective Porter. Are you Delia?"

"Yes, come in." Delia waved Kaila in and shut the door.

"Is anyone else here?" Kaila asked, glancing around the entryway. The white floors seemed to gleam brighter than their yellow walls.

"No. My parents are working."

"Is there somewhere we can talk?"

"Sure. We can go to the living room."

Once they were seated, Kaila began, "About your party...."

"It was terrible what happened to them." Delia sniffed. "They were having a good time."

"When did they arrive?"

"I'm not sure; I think it was about ten o'clock. There were a lot of people."

"Were they there all night?"

"They left around three."

"Together?"

"Yes, they called a cab. They had to prop each other up."

"They had a lot to drink then? Did you see them with anyone specifically?"

"What are you trying to say?" she demanded.

"Nothing, I want to know if there was anyone at the party that was spurned, or followed the girls around, harassing them."

"Oh, OK. Because they're real nice girls. I didn't notice anyone, but I was pretty busy myself."

"Were there any strangers wandering around?"

"Not really, I may not have known them, but I did recognize them from other parties."

"Did you associate often with the girls?"

"Not often. They came with Gerald," Delia answered, crossing her arms as she leaned back.

"Gerald said the girls liked to fool around. Did you see any of their conquests around?"

Delia laughed before saying, "It wasn't like that. They would kiss some guys and maybe a few fondles here and there. But nothing serious. Nothing a guy would get ticked about."

"So there was no one here that night?"

Delia looked away for a moment. "No."

"How do you know Rachel and Victoria?"

"I went to school with all of them."

"Really!" Kaila said with surprise.

"I always get that reaction. I'm only twenty-one." She looked quite proud of herself.

"Did you guys hang out?"

"No. We had different friends."

"If you think of anything please give me a call. Thanks for your time," Kaila said, standing up and handing Delia her card.

"I hope you find the guy quickly." Delia closed the door.

Kaila stared at the door and sighed. *So the party was maybe a dead end; crap!*

Kaila took a detour on the journey back to the station through Tim's. She smiled in pleasure after taking a long sip of her double latte.

As soon as George saw Kaila walking into the station, he asked, "How did it go?"

Kaila groaned. "Rotten. There was nothing. No one suspicious, everything was great and the girls left drunk together in a cab. Delia's recount is completely different than Gerald's. What the girls were doing was harmless and could never be construed as anything else."

George snorted. "She isn't a guy."

The rest of the afternoon Kaila wrote a list of the girls' friends and family to interview and compared the two to see any commonalities. Kaila was grasping at straws, but one of them could be the killer.

Kaila was never so glad to see the end of her shift. She felt more exhausted than when the shift had started. It was nice working twelve-hour shifts though; there was no real rush hour traffic to worry about. Days like these, it would be difficult to sit in her car staring at all the cars piled in front of her. That's when road rage builds up and every little thing becomes extremely annoying. Kaila heard about it all the time from the traffic cops at the station. There is one driver screaming and ranting at another and soon a fight ensues. Some of her friends had to commute an hour to get home.

Holly was sleeping in front of the T.V. with Echo in her lap when Kaila stumbled into the apartment. He didn't even get up, *the traitor,* Kaila thought as she sagged into a chair with a sigh.

"How's work going?" Holly asked, sleepily rubbing her eyes.

"Well, two best friends are dead."

"I heard one of the more experienced did the second autopsy. The word around the water cooler is that it's a serial killer."

"Hopefully no reporter hears them—that would be just what we need."

"Your mom called to see how you're doing."

"I haven't phoned in a while. I should have expected a call. Now it's going to be hard to explain I'm just busy, that there is nothing wrong." Kaila sighed again.

"She wants to be part of your life, Kaila."

"I know. But we've never had a close relationship. So I don't think to call her about every little thing. How's your mom doing?" Kaila said, trying to change the subject.

"Great. A little lonely now that I'm gone. But she started dating someone."

"That's wonderful!" Kaila could remember when Holly and her mom first moved to Cremona. Holly's dad had been abusive so her mom was very gun-shy. Kaila couldn't remember Holly ever talking about her mom dating. *This guy better treat her good,* she thought.

"Yeah. From what she has said, he seems to be nice. I'm glad she's found someone to spend time with. I always worry about her being alone for so long. Growing up, she had me to worry about, but now there's nothing to occupy her time." Holly laughed. "So when's your next day off?"

"Probably not till this weekend. I'm thinking of going home to see Mom and Dad and maybe visit Justin's grave. If I can hold her off that long," Kaila said dryly.

"Have you been out there since you moved?"

"No. I almost feel bad that I forget about him for longer periods of time. When it first happened, I couldn't stop thinking about him and went to his grave every couple of weeks. Now it's like he never existed sometimes and then I remember and feel horrible."

Holly was silent for a moment before saying, "Kaila, that's normal. You're alive; you have to move on. There's no shame in that and I'm sure he wouldn't want you to feel that way."

"I know in my head, but I can't really help it. Hopefully it continues to fade, because I want to remember Justin with a happy feeling."

"Well, say hi to your folks for me. I'm headed off to bed." Holly extracted herself from the sleeping Echo and dropped him into Kaila's lap.

"Why so early?"

"I have an exam in the morning and I think I'm getting sick."

"Well, hopefully you'll feel better. Good luck tomorrow."

For a while, all Kaila could think of was Justin. She had difficulties picturing him now, other than his last moments. His surprised expression as Jade's gun went off and the pain he must have felt as he fell to the ground. Their eyes had met one last time before the life just left them. If Kaila hadn't been in such bad shape, she might have done something to Jade she would have later regretted, maybe. Kaila shook herself out of her reprieve and grabbed the remote off the coffee table and began flipping channels. There must be a good movie on one of them; there was no way sleep would be coming easy now.

Chapter 13

Kaila dragged herself into the station the next morning. Sleep had been elusive and she'd watched T.V. until late into the morning. Echo didn't help, because as soon as her head hit the pillow and her eyes closed, he began whimpering. As any dog owner has probably learned, trying to sleep with a wiggling puppy? Not so easy. So, as she tossed and turned in bed, Echo would wake and try to play.

Of course George was already there. She wouldn't be getting a leg up on him for a while.

"Kaila, you look like shit," George commented dryly.

"Thanks. I didn't sleep well last night."

"That's what happens when you let your boyfriend in," George razzed as he laughed.

"Very funny. What do we have?"

"A whole lot of nothing. We still need check out Rachel's work, and might as well stop at Victoria's."

"Do we know where she worked?"

"Rachel worked at the Copper Kettle and Victoria was at Road's Veterinarian."

"Really, Victoria's job surprises me."

"We'll head out around eight-thirty so we arrive when they open. Let's make time for a stop at Tim's. I know I'm going to need a large coffee," George said.

"That sounds good." Kaila nodded her head in agreement before turning back to her computer and pulling up her notes.

After picking up drinks, their first stop was the veterinarian's. Loud noise greeted them as they opened the doors. The waiting room was full with mostly dogs and a few cats. Peering around the room, Kaila noticed how many of the pets looked similar to their owners; hopefully she and Echo didn't start looking alike; it would put a crimp in her dating. Kaila giggled at this and George glanced her way, a question in his eyes and she just waved him off. They walked up to the counter and Kaila showed her badge as she addressed the harried looking woman behind. "Hello, can we speak to the doctor about Victoria?"

The receptionist's eyes welled up with tears before she said, "That was just awful. Everyone loved her here. We're pretty busy, but I'll see if he has time."

"We really need to talk with him; it's not an option," George stated.

The woman looked at him with surprise before spinning around and stomping out of the room. A few minutes later she came back and said, "Follow me."

They were led to a small office in the back where a rather large man sat behind a desk. He was built like a giant, stocky boxer dog, square, with all of his hair only to be found in his full mustache and beard. The doctor's head glittered from the sun shining through the window behind him as he bent over writing furiously on a notepad.

"Hello, detectives, please sit down. I don't have much time to talk, as you could probably see from my waiting room."

"This shouldn't take long. We just had a few questions about Victoria," Kaila said.

"I'll try to answer what I can, but I'm not sure how much help I'll be."

"How long did Victoria worked here?" George asked.

"On and off for about three years."

"So she was a good worker?" Kaila asked.

"Yes. She helped me out in the examinations. Victoria was deciding if veterinarian medicine could be her career. She wanted to learn as much as she could."

"Do you know if she had any problems with any of the staff here or the customers?" George questioned.

"Of course not. Everyone adored Victoria; she was a wonderful girl. Her compassion for the animals was extensive, and the owners could see this. There is only me, Wanda at the front and Victoria."

"Did she bring any of her friends here?"

"Not that I saw, but you could ask Wanda. Now, if that's all, I need to get going," the doctor said, standing up. They followed suit and headed back to the front. Kaila could feel his eyes staring at them as they walked down the hall. Wanda was nowhere to be seen so they waited a few minutes and questioned her before leaving the office.

"Well, that gave us squat," George said.

"Maybe we'll have more luck at the Copper Kettle." Kaila climbed into the truck. It was rush hour traffic so by the time they reached the restaurant George was muttering under his breath about drivers in the city. His hands clenched the steering wheel as he stared straight ahead.

"OK, let's get this done," George muttered as he stomped to the front door.

The restaurant was full and they had to wait a few minutes before a waitress hurried towards them.

"For how many?" she asked quickly.

"We would like to talk with the manager," Kaila said.

"Oh. I think he's busy right now." She whipped her head around, glancing throughout the room.

"Please find him, this is important," George said as he flashed his badge.

Her eyes grew big as she nodded and hiked towards the back. Kaila flopped down on one of the benches and closed her eyes.

"Are you going to make it?" George laughed as he watched her.

"Yes, I'm just resting my eyes."

"I've heard that one before."

Kaila stuck out her tongue and smiled as she continued to rest. They waited for about ten minutes before a man walked up to them. "My name is Peter Copperfield, the manager. How can I help you?"

"Do you have somewhere we can talk in private?" George asked.

"Sure, follow me."

Peter gestured to the empty chairs and sat behind his desk, staring at them with a curious expression.

"We're here about Rachel," Kaila stated.

"Oh, yes. We heard about the terrible accident. Why would you be here for that?"

Kaila looked at George in surprise before she responded, "Rachel wasn't in an accident; she was murdered."

"What! That's horrible. Who did it?"

"We are investigating right now. Can we ask you questions about her work," George said.

"Sure, sure."

"Were there any problems with the staff or customers?"

114

"Just the usual."

"What do you mean by that?"

"Well, there are teenagers working here, so you get all the drama that goes along with them. And of course there are always the customers that have small issues, but not enough to kill someone."

"Do you mind if we talk to the rest of the staff?"

"You can talk to them if they're not busy."

"What shifts did Rachel usually work?"

"She was working second and third shift."

"Can I ask why you thought she was in an accident?"

"Her parents told me."

Both Kaila and George nodded and Kaila said, "Thanks, we will see you later."

They left Peter sitting at the desk staring off into space.

"Why would they tell him that?" Kaila whispered.

"I'm not sure; maybe they don't want all the questions?"

"Well, let's split up and question the rest," Kaila suggested, heading towards the kitchen.

Kaila pushed open the doors and quickly sidestepped as a cook ran by carrying two trays of food. There was a cook in the corner mixing salads and three cooks on the line calling out orders and plating food on large white plates.

"Excuse me," a server said, glancing at Kaila with a question in her eyes as she hurried by juggling a pile of dirty dishes.

Kaila walked over to the salad cook and asked, "Can I ask you a few questions?" flashing her badge. He glanced over in surprise as he kept flipping a salad with his tongs.

"I'm pretty busy."

"This won't take long. I have a few questions about Rachel."

"Alright, but I need to keep working."

"Sure."

"Where is that salad?" a voice yelled out.

"Here it is," the cook ran over to the counter.

Kaila waited for his return and then asked, "How well did you know Rachel?"

"Not very, I've only worked here for about six months."

"You look about the same age; you never hung out, went to the same parties?"

"Not really, we didn't hang out with the same crowds." He walked away again with another plate.

"What about the other employees? Did she spend any time with anyone else here?"

"Some of us would go out for drinks after work and Rachel stayed for one or two before buggering off."

"Did you see any staff or customers bothering her?"

"Like how?"

"I don't know, following her, asking her out."

"Not that I saw, just the regular stuff. But I'm stuck in the back here."

"What's regular stuff?"

"There're always customers hitting on the girls, but they back down once they're told no. What's with all these questions, I thought she died in a car accident?"

"No, she was murdered," Kaila said softly.

He looked taken aback. "What! How did it happen?"

"We're not sure at the moment; the investigation is still ongoing."

Kaila was able to talk with a few other cooks before she left to find George.

"So, let's compare notes," George said, as they sat at their desks.

"Everyone I talked to was surprised how Rachel died and had no idea. I guess everyone thought there had been an accident," Kaila answered.

"A few of the waitresses hated Rachel and couldn't care less that she's gone. I can't believe how petty girls are; I know you weren't like that, right?"

"Of course not. There were girls like that in school, though; I wouldn't trust them as far as I could throw them."

"And everyone else was no help. It was the normal customer complaints, nothing vicious, I'm told."

"OK, so we are no closer to solving these murders than in the beginning, other than to clear our one good suspect. Right?" Kaila sighed and dropped her head to her desk.

"Maybe we need to talk to their parents again. See if there's any connection through them." George suggested.

"I'll call Rachel's place," Kaila said, grabbing the phone.

After a few rings, a woman answered. "Walker residence."

"Hello, this is Detective Kaila Porter, is either Mr. or Mrs. Walker there?"

A short pause and then the woman said, "No, they went on a trip."

"What! Why did they go? Where?"

Kaila watched as George started waving his hands, trying to get her attention.

"I'm sorry; I don't know where they went. I think I heard them mention that the trip was planned a while ago."

"Can I please get their cell number?"

Kaila furiously wrote as the housekeeper gave her the number and then hung up.

"What the hell is going on?" George demanded.

"I can't believe it. They went on a trip."

"Are they insane? What's their problem? Their daughter was murdered. Who in the hell goes on a trip at this time?"

"I don't know. I'll try and call them."

Kaila let their cell phone continue ringing until finally it went to a generic voice message.

"No answer," Kaila said frustrated. "How're we going to continue the investigation when Rachel's parents are gone?"

"I haven't a clue. Mr. Bates better still be in town, or our case could be stalled. And I'll be very suspicious on why they all flew the coop."

"You can't really think they had something to do with this?"

"What else are we supposed to think? If it was anyone else involved with the victim we would probably be thinking that."

"I just can't fathom parents' killing their children," Kaila said, horrified.

"I didn't say they did it, but maybe they are involved."

"Well, I'm calling Mr. Bates, and if he's there, we go right over before he disappears. We can stop by Mr. Walker's office and talk with the secretary, and maybe some of their family knows what's going on."

"I'm so glad he's still here," Kaila said, knocking on the door.

A haggard Mr. Bates opened the door. He didn't look like he'd shaved since Monday and he stared at the detectives with bloodshot eyes.

"Have you found my daughter's killer?" he demanded.

"Not yet, as I said on the phone, we just have a few more questions for you," Kaila said. "Can we come in?"

"I guess." Mr. Bates waved them in and proceeded to the living room. "Ask your questions."

"Have you heard from Mr. and Mrs. Walker?" Kaila asked.

"What does this have to do with Victoria?" Mr. Bates demanded.

"We're not sure yet, but they left town and went on a holiday."

"Oh, I remember them talking about going a couple of weeks back. I guess they didn't want to lose their money."

"Can you think of anyone that would want to harm you? So far in our investigation we haven't found anyone connected to Victoria."

"I sometimes have upset clients who don't like their homes, but they wouldn't harm my little girl. It has to be some stalker out there, some pyscho."

"Was Victoria seeing anyone right now? Does she have any close friends from school?"

"She was seeing some guy a while back, but he wasn't good enough for her and they broke up. Her only real friend had been Rachel."

"Do you know why she never brought anyone else around here?" George asked.

Mr. Bates looked surprised as he responded, "She never talked about any other girls, or asked to have them over."

"No one else you can think of? Would you know where her yearbooks are? Maybe we can find some friends in there."

"I wouldn't have a clue where to start," Mr. Bates said.

"Do you mind if we look in her room? Anything we can find may help find her killer," Kaila implored.

She could already see him shutting down. He was starting to fidget and wouldn't make eye contact.

"I don't know. Do you really need to?"

"Yes, it would be a great help," George interjected.

"I guess. Follow me. Make sure you don't mess anything up. I will be downstairs waiting." The detectives watched as Mr. Bates walked back down the stairs before turning to face Victoria's room. It looked like she had never grown up, or hadn't been allowed to.

The room was huge; it could probably fit Kaila's living room and kitchen. A pink four-poster bed was in one corner and a matching pink dresser was sitting close by.

"Oh my god, everything is pink. It would drive me nuts!" Kaila whispered.

"Let's hurry up, it's giving me the willies being in this place," George said, heading for the bookshelf.

They made quick work of it and they found Victoria's yearbooks. There were no secret boxes hidden under the bed or in the corner. The closet only contained hanging clothes arranged by color and neatly organized shelves. It didn't seem like there was a computer either, which was a miracle considering the age they lived in.

Kaila carried the books down the stairs towards Mr. Bates who was standing in the foyer waiting for them.

"What's that?"

"We found her yearbooks, do you mind if we take them? We will bring them back," Kaila asked.

"I guess. Just don't wreck them."

"Did Victoria have a computer?" George inquired.

"No, she used the one in the study."

Kaila looked surprised. "Can we take it?"

"How long will you have it? I have confidential things on there."

"We are just looking for Victoria's emails and history. It could point to a suspect."

"I guess. Just give me a minute." Mr. Bates left them in the foyer for at least ten minutes.

"What is taking him so long?" Kaila whispered.

George shrugged his shoulders and stared in the direction that Mr. Bates had left.

Mr. Bates finally strode in carrying the laptop.

"Thanks," George said, accepting the laptop. "We will return it after our IT department has looked through it."

Mr. Bates followed closely behind and shut the door immediately after them.

Chapter 14

Back at the station, they began the tedious task of going through the yearbooks.

"She wasn't in any clubs this year," Kaila commented. "And she doesn't look real happy either."

"In this one, too. She has one comment that's a little vicious."

"From who?" Kaila asked, leaning to read over George's shoulder.

"It's not signed, of course."

"'...hope you're kicked out of this school, you don't belong. Or maybe just die and it'll solve everything....' Crap! Who would write something like that?" Kaila asked.

"I wonder if she told anyone about this?"

"Which year was that?" Kaila asked.

George flipped the book over searching for a date, "Oh, here it is. Grade eleven."

"Do you think the principal will remember?"

"Wouldn't hurt to pay a visit, if they're anything like mine growing up; my principal had a memory like an elephant," George suggested.

"Alright, how about you talk with Mr. Bates to check if he saw this, and I'll stop at the school."

"Fine."

Kaila recalled her years signing friends' books. It was a great part of the high school experience. Of course, there were sometimes inappropriate comments, but nothing like Victoria's.

She looked up the address to St. Peter's school and then headed out. The drive would probably take thirty minutes and it was almost the end of the school day. She'd better book it.

Kaila pulled up to a gorgeous black and brown brick building. There were plenty of windows facing the street and a large school sign hung over the doors. Bushes grew under each window and trees spotted the grounds in front. *It must be very pretty during the summer*, Kaila thought, walking up to the doors. She wandered in the halls until a student recognized a lost person and directed her to the office.

"Hello, is the principal in?" Kaila asked, showing her badge to the secretary.

"Just a minute, I'll check if she's free. Can I ask what this is in regards to?"

"I have a few questions about some previous students."

While she waited, Kaila looked over the graduating class pictures hung in the office. She spotted Rachel and Victoria's just as the woman entered.

"Mrs. Schmidt will see you."

The woman waiting behind the desk reminded Kaila of every stereotype told about a principal. Her hair was pulled back in a severe bun, and her pointed glasses perched on the end of her nose. Kaila could feel her gaze pierce through her as Mrs. Schmidt stood up and offered her hand.

"Hello, Detective. What can I help you with?"

"My name is Detective Kaila Porter. Can I ask you a few questions about Rachel Walker and Victoria Bates? They attended here a few years ago."

"Sure, I remember them. It is horrible what happened to them."

"We were looking through Victoria's yearbooks and found in her Grade Eleven an inappropriate comment. There was no name signed, but it said: 'Hope you're kicked out of this school, you don't belong. Or maybe just die and it'll solve everything.' Did Victoria say anything to you?"

"That's terrible, no, I didn't hear anything," she said with a gasp. "But of course Victoria was a very private girl and I'm not sure she would have told anyone."

"Did you notice anyone picking on Victoria, or did she ever complain about a classmate?"

"She never pointed a finger. Once in a while Victoria would end up in the nurse's office with cuts or bruises."

"You don't think they were because of clumsiness or accidents?"

"No, not that many times. But, of course, getting her to open up was impossible."

"Did she have any other friends?"

"Just Rachel that I noticed. She was shy and kept to herself. That's probably why Victoria became a target for the popular girls to harass."

"Did you inform her father?"

"Of course, but he just said that was part of growing up. Mr. Bates did promise to talk with Victoria about it."

"Did you have any suspicions of who was hurting her?"

"Yes. There was a group of girls led by Delia that ensured the unwanted riffraff didn't stick around."

"Unwanted?" Kaila asked in surprise.

"I heard them talking once. Of course, I pulled them into my office, but I don't think it helped."

"That's funny, because I just talked with a Delia and the girls were at her party this past weekend."

"Well, if Rachel was there that might explain things. It was because of Rachel that Victoria didn't receive worse punishments from those girls."

"So Rachel didn't seem to have problems?"

"No, even though she didn't run with Delia's crowd, everyone liked her. Not sure how Rachel accomplished that."

"Did all the girls attend high school for the four years?"

"Yes."

"Thanks for your time. Is the same nurse still working here?"

"Yes. Mrs. Tiller should still be around. I'll take you to her." Mrs. Schmidt rose from behind her desk and motioned Kaila to follow. As they were walking through the halls, the last bell rang and the classrooms spilled out, surrounding them. Kaila tried keeping up as they waded through the throngs of youth hurrying to their lockers. They finally reached a door with 'School Nurse' stamped across the frosted glass and Mrs. Schmidt entered.

"Hello, Mrs. Tiller. Detective Porter has some questions about Victoria Bates. Do you remember her?"

"Of course I do. Come in, Detective, don't just stand there."

"I'll leave you in capable hands," Mrs. Schmidt said to Kaila.

"Thanks for your help. If you think of anything else, please give me a call," Kaila said, handing over her card.

"I will. I hope you catch the bastard," she snarled.

Kaila looked at her in surprise, never expecting those words to spill out. Kaila then turned around and faced Mrs. Tiller. She looked to be in her late fifties, but seemed quite spry for her age.

"What would you like to know, Detective?"

"I heard that Victoria was in here often with cuts or bruises?"

"That poor dear." She tsked. "I tried to do the best I could."

"I'm sure you did. Do you remember Victoria ever saying what happened?"

Mrs. Tiller leaned back in her chair, a frown developing on her brow. "I don't recall any names, but I had my suspicions."

"Was it another student? Or was she coming to school like that?"

"Oh no, it happened here. I suspected the crowd that ran with a girl named Delia."

"Why did you think that? Did you see something?"

"No. But I observed them interacting together, and it wasn't healthy. That's for sure."

"Did you notice anyone else that bothered Victoria?"

"Not that I can remember. But my memory isn't as good as it used to be." Mrs. Tiller laughed.

"What about Rachel Walker. Did you have much contact with her?"

"Only when she showed up with Victoria, or to get her. Those girls were as thick as thieves. I heard Rachel once whisper to Victoria to tell. I assumed it was about who was hurting her."

"Thanks, Mrs. Tiller. I'll get out of your hair."

"No trouble, dearie."

The halls were long cleared out and Kaila just saw a few scattered pieces of paper left on the floor. She headed back to the office to inspect the graduating classes. It wasn't surprising Victoria stared back with a frown and Delia seemed to shine out from the picture.

Rachel was at the end of the class, a large smile on her face. Kaila waved to the secretary as she left. *It's time to discover what Delia has to say about high school*, Kaila thought with determination. She would stop at the station and let George know what the principal said.

"Well?" George called as Kaila walked in.

"The principal remembered both girls. Victoria never said anything about her yearbook. Once in a while she would end up in the nurse's office. Victoria withheld the name of the culprit. I don't know why she would want to protect girls like that. I also had the chance to talk with the nurse. She didn't have anything new."

"If you snitch, you need to be willing to handle the consequences. I don't think Victoria was strong enough from what I've seen. What about Rachel?"

"Those two were always together, but it didn't look like Rachel was bullied at all."

"Did they go there for all four years?"

"Yup. What about Victoria's dad?"

"He was shocked. Victoria never told him anything or showed him the book."

"Wasn't he suspicious about all the trips to the nurse's office?"

"He didn't mention anything about that."

"That's surprising. The principal said Mr. Bates was told about Victoria's injuries."

"Maybe he didn't think they were from bullying."

Kaila shook her head, "I think it's terrible, and guess who our bully was? Though it's a long stretch to go from yearbook nasty to murder."

"Not a clue."

"Delia, our party host."

"Really!"

"I was going to head over now. Do you want to come? I want to discover why she left out making Victoria's life hell."

"Sounds like a plan. I'm driving," George stated, grabbing his coat.

Of course. Kaila smiled, following behind.

"Did you discover any other friends?" George asked.

"No. Rachel was liked by everyone and Delia's crowd never harassed her. Victoria was another story; even though she never pointed a finger, it was suspected that Delia had a hand in it."

"Were there any witnesses to the harassment?"

"No. They only suspected, so couldn't do anything about it."

"That's too bad."

Kaila pounded on Delia's door and stepped back to wait. Delia answered a few minutes later with a breathless voice. "Yes?"

"Hello, Delia, do you have a few minutes? I have some more questions."

"I don't have much time, I was just heading out."

"It won't take long."

Delia sighed before opening the door wider, and said, "I guess."

"This is Detective Hapner, my partner."

"Hello," said George.

Delia nodded in his direction before leading them to the living room.

"What do you want to know?" Delia asked.

"I wanted to know about high school. You were supposedly in the cool group—and Victoria was unwanted riffraff?"

Delia opened and closed her mouth, no sound emanating. Kaila wasn't sure if Delia was going to answer. "That was long time ago," she finally said softly, wringing her hands and looking at the floor.

"Not really, only a couple of years. So, you're friends now? She was invited to your party. Did you guys hang out?"

"No, like I said before, she came with Gerald. But I'm different now. It was wrong how we acted in high school. I apologized to Victoria and she was OK with it."

"What about the other girls in your group. Do they regret their actions?"

"I don't really associate with them anymore, but if you're implying that they could have done this, I don't think so. They couldn't have killed someone."

"Sometimes it's the most unlikely person. Where were you Sunday night?" Kaila asked.

"What! Are you accusing me of killing her?" Delia screeched, standing up.

"No. We have to ask everyone so you can be eliminated as a suspect and we can continue searching for the real one."

Delia's body was shaking as she slumped back into her chair, crossing her arms. George had not spoken or moved the whole time. He just stared at Delia, watching her every movement.

"So, what were you doing?" Kaila asked again.

"I was at home, with my parents." Delia frowned and fingered the edge of her shirt.

"The whole night?"

"Yes."

"Are your parents here right now?"

"No. They went out for dinner with friends. They probably won't be home for a couple of hours."

"Do they work Monday to Friday?"

"Yes."

"Can you write down where they work and the numbers?" Kaila asked, handing over her pad.

"Why do you have to bother them at work?" Delia demanded. "Can't it wait?"

"I'm sorry, but no. We need to continue with the investigation as quickly as possible."

Kaila could see that a few tears had welled up in Delia's eyes and wondered if they were real or for their benefit.

Delia furiously scribbled down the information and then stood up, pointing to the door. "I'd like you to leave now."

Kaila and George slowly stood up and headed for the door.

"Thanks for your—" before Kaila could finish, Delia slammed the door in their faces.

"That went well," George said sarcastically, walking down the step. "A little suspicious."

"She hasn't changed *that* much, has she? But I don't know if she would have been strong enough to kill the girls," Kaila said. "I'm sure you noticed she isn't a big girl."

"What are you talking about, I didn't see anything."

She just shook her head, climbing into the truck. "First thing tomorrow we should try and talk with her parents."

"I'm sure Delia will have already prepped them about what to say."

"Well, let's hope it's the truth or things could get ugly."

They pulled up to the station and George idled by the door. "I better get home; tonight the wife is having people over. If I'm not there to help, I'll get hell."

"See you tomorrow." Kaila laughed.

The first thing Kaila did the next morning upon reaching the station was to call Delia's parents. Mr.

Morgan answered the phone after the first ring, like he was waiting for the call.

"Hello, is this Mr. Morgan?"

"Yes. Who wants to know?"

"My name is Detective Porter. I talked with Delia yesterday."

"She told me what you accused her of."

"Do you have time for us to come by and ask you and your wife a few questions?"

"We don't know anything about any murders."

"Please, this will help with the investigation."

There was a pause on the phone. "Delia said you got our work information. I guess you can stop by today and ask. We have to leave soon."

"Thanks. See you later." Kaila hung up the phone in triumph and turned towards George. "We can question them at work today."

"Great! Where do they work?" George asked.

"Let me look." Kaila scrambled to find her notes from the previous day with Delia. "Here they are." Kaila held out her notebook and scanned her scribbles until she reached Delia's writing. "Hey, George, quick, grab me that yearbook of Victoria's," Kaila said excitedly.

George looked at her in surprise, but jumped up and searched his desk for the book.

"What am I looking for?" George demanded.

"That anonymous writing," Kaila said pointing at her pad.

George flipped to the back of the yearbook and brought it over.

"Doesn't that writing look awfully close to Delia's?" Kaila questioned, glancing between the two.

George bent over examining the notepad with Delia's writing. "You know, I think you could be right. Our mystery person is Delia; that doesn't look good for her."

"I know. I hope her parents can provide an alibi for her. We might have to check back to the night Rachel went missing."

"So, what do her parents do?" George asked.

"Her mom is a nurse at the Foothills Medical Centre and Mr. Morgan works at Mark's Work Warehouse."

"Really. That's a surprise. How could they have afforded to send Delia to St. Peter's? It's expensive there."

"Maybe that's why their house is so modest. They used all their disposable income for Delia's education."

"That's possible."

Kaila worked on typing up her notes from the interviews yesterday until they left to chat with Mr. and Mrs. Morgan.

Their first stop was the hospital since it was close to the station. They stopped at the desk and flashed their badges, inquiring about Mrs. Morgan. The nurse gestured to an empty room to wait until she arrived. They ended up having to wait for almost half an hour and George was ready to explode.

"I'm sorry about the wait," a tall, skinny woman said, rushing into the room. "I was with a patient and couldn't leave until the doctor arrived."

"We understand," Kaila said, cutting off George.

"I'm Detective Porter and this is Detective Hapner. Can we ask you a few questions about Sunday night?"

"What do you want to know? We were with Delia all night," she defended.

"You're sure neither of you left even for a bit?" Kaila asked.

Mrs. Morgan crossed her arms and frowned at them. "No. We ate supper around six o'clock, watched a movie, and then Delia went to her room."

"So you never saw her after that?" Kaila inquired.

"What do you mean? I heard her up there, she was playing her music."

"But you never spoke to her again or saw her?"

"She was there, I swear!" Mrs. Morgan said, shaking her head. "She couldn't have left, I would have seen her."

"Where were you during the night?"

"Both my husband and myself were in the living room watching T.V. So we would have heard her leaving out the front."

"From what I observed, your couch and chairs face away from the door. Isn't it possible that she could have snuck out? Or do you have a back door?" Kaila demanded.

"No, no, you are twisting everything around. My girl is a sweet thing, she wouldn't have done anything."

"What about in high school?" George questioned.

"What about it?" Mrs. Morgan was almost in tears and rubbing her hands up and down her arms.

"We heard that Delia had some trouble with Victoria at school, bullying."

"That was just a vicious rumour. It was those girls Delia hung out with. We told her they were trouble. But she wouldn't listen."

"Here, Mrs. Morgan, have a seat. We're just trying to discover who murdered Rachel and Victoria," Kaila said, gently guiding her to a chair before she fell.

"I don't understand what's happening here. How can you think Delia killed those girls, she isn't like that."

"We want to clear her name, that's all."

Mrs. Morgan looked at them skeptically before pulling a tissue out of her pocket and dabbing her eyes. "Well, I think if you want to talk with me anymore, I should have a lawyer." She stood up and stormed out of the room, leaving them in her wake.

"Let's hurry to Mr. Morgan's work. I doubt we can beat her calling him," George said, rushing out.

George was snarling by the time they pulled into the parking lot. The traffic had been horrendous and they were sure he would be unwilling to talk with them.

"Let's get this over with," George grumbled.

For being early morning there were quite a few customers milling around the store. They walked up to the counter and Kaila asked, "Can we please speak with Mr. Morgan?"

"I'll see if he's busy. Just a minute." The girl slowly ambled through the store to the back corner and disappeared. *I wonder if she could have walked any slower?* Kaila thought.

It wasn't long before she reappeared followed by a rather tall man with a huge black mustache. It was almost to the point of being a handlebar mustache.

"Come this way," he demanded and headed back the way he came.

"I've talked with my wife and I don't appreciate your insinuations. I know you have a job to do, but leave my family out of it. She has already said we were all home Sunday night."

"I'm sorry if this is uncomfortable, Mr. Morgan, but it isn't looking great for Delia. All we need to do is clear up where she was Sunday. Delia is potentially right in the middle of this. We have discovered some interesting things from their high school days and she recently interacted with the victims."

"What about high school? That was years ago." He crossed his arms and eyed them warily.

"We just need to know in your words what happened this past Sunday," Kaila said.

"Fine. We had supper, watched a movie and then Delia went upstairs."

"Do you recall what time that was?"

Mr. Morgan rocked back and forth on his heels as he glared at the detectives. "I think it was nine. *Law and Order* had just started."

"Do you know if she came down or left at any time?"

"Not when we were downstairs."

"How can you be sure?" George asked.

"Because we have a couple of stairs that squeak. I've been meaning to fix them, but haven't gotten around to them. So we'd have heard Delia leaving." His face was smug. "And we didn't go to bed until midnight. I think if you have any other questions for us, you can talk with our lawyer," Mr. Morgan declared and left them, heading to a back office, and slammed the door.

"Well, should we run over and see if Delia is home?" Kaila asked with a grin.

"Damn right!"

They hurried out to the truck and made it in record time to the Morgan's house.

"Do you think she's here?" George asked.

"Let's hope so."

Kaila banged on the door until it swung open, leaving her hand hanging there, and Delia was glaring from the doorway.

"Hello, Delia, can we come in, please. It won't take long at all," Kaila implored.

"Are you going to accuse me again?" she demanded.

"We're trying to get to the bottom of two girls' murders," George answered, his impatience evident.

"Didn't you talk with my parents?"

"Yes, we just want to confirm a few things, and then we're gone," Kaila said.

"Fine," Delia huffed after a few seconds and stepped aside.

They reached the living room, but before sitting down, Kaila asked, "Do you mind if I use the bathroom?"

"I guess. It's the first door on the right up the stairs."

Kaila glanced a minute at George as she turned slowly to face the stairs. There was a black iron railing snaking up the stairs ending with a large post and the steps were dark brown hardwood. She was half way up when a step squeaked quietly. Kaila frowned and took another. This time the noise was louder and she was sure George would hear.

The bathroom was plain, with a tub, shower and pedestal sink. The walls were painted bright yellow with a green wallpaper border. Opening the medicine cabinet and other drawers produced nothing exciting and Kaila flushed the toilet and turned on the water for a moment before leaving. Proceeding down the steps, she treaded as quietly as possible, but those couple of spots still squeaked, making her wince.

"Thanks for your time, Delia. We'll be going." George stood up as Kaila entered the room.

"Whatever," Delia said, marching towards the door and pulling it open with such force that the pictures rattled close by.

Once they were safely in the truck Kaila spun to George and asked, "So, did you hear? Both times."

"Yes."

"Damn. So unless her parents are lying for her, Delia isn't our killer. They'd have heard her descending the stairs. We're back to square one," Kaila said with a frown.

Kaila walked into the station the next morning and slumped at her desk. Sleep had been elusive again as the two girls seemed to dance in front of her eyes.

Straightening up, she began typing her report from yesterday's excitement. They had arrived late at the station and neither she nor George had felt like staying. Kaila was halfway through transcribing when George arrived carrying two large coffees.

"Is that for me? Thanks," Kaila said with a smile, reaching for the coffee.

"I'm not sure, are you done with the reports?" George joked, holding the cup out of her reach.

"If I don't receive caffeine immediately, I might forget how to type and it will fall upon you to finish."

"Fine, fine," George said, quickly passing over the coffee.

Kaila took a sip gingerly before sighing with pleasure. "Are we heading out to Mr. Walker's office? Maybe his secretary knows where they are."

"Sounds like a plan. We'll wait till the report is done." George grinned, facing his desk.

Kaila stuck her tongue out in his direction before continuing her typing.

Before long they were trying to navigate through the rush hour traffic inch by inch. Mr. Walker's office was in the heart of downtown Calgary, close to the Calgary Tower. They rode the elevator up to the eighteenth floor and stepped off to face a large, double-glass door with a young lady on the other side.

"Hello, can I help you?" she asked as they pushed open the heavy doors.

"Yes, can we ask you a few questions?" Kaila flashed her badge.

"Oh." She looked surprised. "I guess, I'm kind of busy though."

George looked around the empty room with skepticism.

"Did Mr. Walker go on a holiday?" Kaila asked.
"Yes."

"Do you know when the trip was planned? Was it last minute?"

"I don't think so. If I recall, he mentioned the trip weeks ago."

"Do you know where they went?"

"Let me check his calendar." She typed a minute on the computer before saying, "No, it doesn't say."

"He didn't let you know in case there was an emergency?" George asked with surprise.

"I can call his cell if required."

"Can you please try now?" Kaila asked.

"I guess. Why am I calling?"

"We just have a few questions about his daughter's case and he's not answering."

The secretary slowly picked up her phone and dialed. Kaila could hear the ringing echo in the room. The secretary was hanging up when a voice connected, saying, "Hello."

"Hi, Mr. Walker." She quickly pulled the phone back to her ear.

She nodded a few times while listening and then said, "The detectives are trying to contact you. ...Mr. Walker...Mr. Walker...." she looked at the receiver and then up at Kaila. "I'm sorry, but we lost the connection."

"Did he say where they were?" Kaila demanded.

"No."

"What was he saying?"

"Mr. Walker was giving some instructions about his patients."

"That's it? He didn't ask about his daughter's case?" Kaila questioned.

"No."

"Please let him know next time you're in communication with him that it's imperative he contacts the police department."

"Alright. Is there anything else?" she asked, looking quickly back at her computer screen.

"Can you think of any patients that were angry with Mr. Walker?"

"Oh no. He's a great doctor. Everyone loved their results," she gushed.

"There were no lawsuits pending?"

"Of course not! Like I said, he had no unhappy clients." She shook her head.

"Thanks for your help. We'll be in touch." George turned towards the door.

"When we get back to the station, we should probably check the court records for any law suits. I believe his secretary thinks he walks on water," Kaila said, frowning as she punched the elevator button.

"I really don't think there was a bad connection; he didn't want to talk with us. I want to know why," George said.

"Yeah, there's just not something right with that family. I wonder if there are any other family members in Calgary, or if they had traveled from another city," Kaila wondered, thinking about the people they saw at the Walkers' house.

"We need to talk with them as well. Maybe they know why Rachel's parents took off during this crucial time. Let's head back to the station and investigate their relatives."

"Hey, George, Kaila, in here," the captain demanded as they entered the station.

Kaila glanced at George in surprise as the other officers yelled out their opinions on why they were in trouble.

"Yeah, Captain?" George asked.

"I just got a complaint from Mr. Morgan saying the police department is harassing his family?" He stared at them expectantly.

"We're working on a lead in the two murders. Delia, their daughter, has come up during the investigation as a possible suspect and we were interviewing the family."

"Mr. Morgan said he told you to talk with their lawyer, but you went ahead and harassed their daughter again."

"Sorry, sir, but Delia is over eighteen and when Mr. Morgan invoked his rights for a lawyer, he was talking about him and his wife. Delia was nowhere around and he didn't mention her," George answered.

"Alright, but watch yourself with this family. We don't need a lawsuit. How did the talk go with Delia?"

"We're thinking that she couldn't have committed the second murder. Unless she crawled out a window," Kaila said with a sigh.

"Are there any other suspects?"

"Not yet," Kaila said.

"Alright, get out of here. I have things to do," the captain said before turning back to his computer.

"Surprise, surprise," Kaila muttered as she stepped up to her desk. "I am starting to find that family very irritating."

"Don't let it get to you. It happens quite often," George said as he followed behind her.

"Are you going to research the family and I'll check for law suits?" Kaila asked with a groan.

"Sure. Either one involves me turning on this heap of junk."

Kaila laughed as George glared at the offending electronic sitting in front of him.

She pulled up the court database and began searching Mr. Walker for any action commenced, or in progress. Kaila drummed her fingers on the desk as her computer began to think. *Great*, Kaila thought. About five minutes later her computer binged and her results showed nothing. *I wonder about concluded or dismissed.* She typed furiously and pushed send before spinning around to George.

"How's it going?"

"Rachel's aunt and uncle live in town. So far everyone else lives in Edmonton or British Columbia. Have you discovered anything?"

"There are no in progress litigations, just waiting for the technology to show me the concluded ones, if any." Just then a bell sounded behind her. "Well, look at this," Kaila said with a smile.

George stood up and looked over her shoulder. Four closed litigations blinked back at them.

"I guess you have a place to start," he said with a grin.

"What are you doing?" Kaila asked.

"I'll be talking to the only family members in town."

"Haha. We'll see about that. I know how much you love driving in the traffic—how about I interview them and you do this research," Kaila cajoled.

"Not a chance." George laughed, grabbing his phone and turned his back to her.

Kaila grimaced before lowering her head and beginning the arduous task of researching the litigations. Who were the plaintiffs, what the complaints and results were.

Three out of the four suits were minor complaints that the plaintiffs lost, but the fourth was a woman that went in for enlarging her lips and cheeks. In the before picture, the woman's lips were thin and severe looking, and her cheeks were chubby. After Mr. Walker was through with her, the woman claimed her life was in ruins; she was harassed constantly by strangers and coworkers. Her lips looked like they had exploded and now took up a good proportion of her face and her new cheek prosthetics were very sharp and uneven. One side was quite close to her eye while the other was noticeably lower on her face. *Was the doctor on something that day?* Kaila wondered, staring at the poor woman. In the end, Mr. Walker's insurance had to pay out a sizable chunk of money to compensate her and cover her future surgeries to fix the mistakes.

Kaila stood up and stretched as her back spasmed from being stationary too long. It was the end of her shift. Tomorrow would be filled with interviewing all the plaintiffs. She began gathering her things, looking around for George, but he hadn't returned. Kaila really wanted to know if anyone knew why Rachel's parents had left. She guessed it would have to wait.

It was going to be another night of searching for food, collapsing on the couch, drifting in and out of consciousness until she dragged her ass to bed. Then staring up at the ceiling for what seemed like the rest of the night. The whole time Echo continually tried to play catch, but to no avail.

The next couple of days Kaila and George were busy interviewing the plaintiffs. They were also baffled that Rachel's parents were still out of town, and no one supposedly had contact with them. They hadn't called to inquire on Rachel's investigation and family members denied having any knowledge other than it was a planned vacation. Kaila was starting to question what kind of parents they were, and why were they gone so long. There was also pressure from the public, as the papers began speculating. Of course there were no basis to any of their thoughts, just allegations.

The police gave a few press releases, but they couldn't talk much about the ongoing investigation. The papers were linking both murders and saying there was a serial killer walking free on the streets of Calgary.

Friday after her shift, Kaila drove home to Cremona. She needed to visit Justin's grave and then her parents. Kaila grabbed the flowers from the front seat and hiked to Justin's resting place. She laid the flowers on his tombstone and sat back on her haunches.

"I miss you, Justin. I hope you're happy where you are. I'm sure you're in a great place. Sorry I haven't been here for a while; it's been crazy at the station. Two girls were killed; they remind me of Holly and me. The case has been difficult and I'm trying to stay objective. We don't really have anything, and I'm worried the killer might get away.

"The apartment Holly and I have is great; we just painted it last weekend. You would have liked it: right by a park so you could run. You could have taken Echo." Kaila laughed. "I better get going, time to see Mom. I know, I know, I need to stay in touch with her more. But you know how we are. I do try." Kaila kissed her fingers and placed them on the tombstone for a minute. She wiped her eyes, stood up and headed to the car.

Her parents' cars were in the driveway when she drove up. Time to face the music; her mother was going to bend her ear for not calling.

Kaila trudged up the steps and tried the door, but it was locked. *Nuts, I forgot to bring my key.* Kaila stood shivering on the steps for a bit before her dad finally opened the door.

"Why are you letting your daughter freeze?" Kaila laughed as her dad enveloped her in a large, warm hug.

"I'm so glad you're here. Why didn't you call?"

"I wasn't sure if I could make it."

"Come in, it's cold out there." Grant dragged Kaila in, slamming the door behind her.

"Is Mom here?"

"Yes, she's in the bedroom. She's been worried about you."

"I know. But I've been good, nothing to report." Kaila walked up the steps to her parents' bedroom and knocked.

"Come in."

Kaila opened the door and peeked in. Her mom stood in front of the closet pulling clothes out, a pile already lying on the bed.

"Hi, Mom. What are you doing?"

"Kaila!" Debbie ran over and squeezed Kaila until she couldn't breathe.

Debbie stood back looking at her with a smile.

"What?" Kaila asked.

"Just getting my fill, you're my only child."

"Oh, enough." Kaila smiled as she gently pushed her mother away. "So, what's going on?" Kaila gestured to the clothes.

"I'm purging. There're way too many clothes in there."

Kaila sifted through the pile. "What are you going to do with them?"

"I'll donate them. Do you want any?"

"Ah, no, that's alright. They're old lady clothes."

"Hey!" Debbie slapped Kaila's hand as she laughed.

"Do you need help?"

"Sure, grab some bags and load them up. Are you staying long?"

"If you haven't eaten yet, I was planning to stay until after supper. Is that alright?"

"Of course, you're always welcome. Our eating habits haven't changed since you left. Your dad is still working later than I would like. I wish you would call more often," she chided.

"I know, Mom, but I'm busy and there's nothing to report. I'll be right back." Kaila escaped before any more questions were fired in her direction.

After supper Debbie shooed Kaila and her dad into the living room as she loaded the dishwasher, saying they had things to discuss. It gave Kaila time to go over the case with her dad and get a different viewpoint.

Darkness had fallen when Kaila pulled out of the driveway with a full stomach and a couple of Tupperware containers. That was one good thing about coming home: great home-cooked food. On the long drive home Kaila had plenty of time to reflect on the atrocities inflicted on the girls. Was it over? Did the killer have someone else in his or her sights? Cases like these were so frustrating with no clear motive. The girls seemed like model citizens; of course, they were young and careless, so model might not be the right word. Kaila laughed for a minute, and then sighed. Tomorrow was another day; maybe she would just head to the station bright and early. Looking through all their notes might give her some ideas. There had to be something they missed. They should probably start looking into the Walker's financing.

Chapter 15

The man stared down at the pictures laid out in front of him. If someone looked around the room they would never know something gruesome had occurred there, much less twice. He slowly stroked his chin and contemplated his next move. *I know, I know. More had to pay.* He wasn't finished with his mission. He yelled to himself, knocking his head, trying to silence *them.*

How could he accomplish the next phase? It would be more difficult. The first two had been quite easy, but he didn't want to become complacent. He also needed to be more careful; he was almost seen with that last one. Grabbing a picture, he picked it up and glared into the face staring back. This kid could ruin everything. That made it essential to strictly follow the steps he laid out. He needed to determine the time and place for the reckoning to begin. He had to finish what he started.

The first thing was to figure out where the kid would be alone. The man wanted to say the name of his next victim, but stopped. It couldn't become personal or he might panic and give in. He would show that stupid bitch of an ex-wife that he wasn't crazy. It hadn't been his fault. Wasn't that her exact words as she left and tore his life apart? 'How could you have been so stupid and lose everything?' He could follow through with something. Maybe he would go and see her next.

A hysterical giggle escaped through his lips before he pushed back his chair. He could hear them agreeing to this new plan. Time to get to work.

Chapter 16

Kaila walked into an almost empty station and sat behind her desk. Her chair scraped across the floor, the sound echoing in the room. She booted up the computer and pulled up the girls' files. They were dropped off at almost the exact same locations. Both were violent and had no sexual assault. They had been friends since early childhood and attended the same schools and club. No real big problems with anyone, other than the bullying at school by Delia and her friends. Both girls were friends with Gerald, but he was a dead end. Same with their work and other friends.

Kaila sat back for a moment and stared at the ceiling. Could it have been a random attack? No, that was hard to believe. They were just starting the investigation into the parents' background. *What could Rachel's parents be doing so long out of town? Were they really vacationing?*

Kaila Googled Mr. and Mrs. Walker, hoping something would pop up. Of course, nothing exciting.

"Maybe it's revenge against the parents." Kaila sighed. It was really time to head home; she needed a break. Monday she would talk with George about the direction of their investigation.

Kaila's first sight walking into the apartment was Holly and Brian necking on the coach.

"Ewww. Come on, guys, I don't need to see that!" Kaila laughed as she ducked into the kitchen.

There was shuffling in the living room, she assumed they were shifting clothes back into place.

"I thought you were gone for the day," Holly said, walking in, a blush staining her cheeks.

"I needed a break, and I'm starved. Hi, Brian."

"Hi, Kaila. How's it going?"

"Not so good, this case is coming to a dead end."

"That's too bad. I hope you catch them soon."

"So do I. I'm worried that the killer isn't done yet."

"Why do you say that?" Holly asked with a frown.

"Not sure, just a feeling. Is there anything to eat in here?" Kaila called from within the fridge.

"Probably not. I haven't had time to shop and I don't think you have either."

"Oh, I forgot about my leftovers." Kaila could feel her mouth start to salivate. *Two good meals in a row, what would her stomach do?* Kaila thought, smiling.

"Do you guys want any?" Kaila slammed the fridge.

"That's fine, it's your food," Holly called.

"Don't be silly. There's plenty. If you want to dish up what you'd like, I'm going to change." Kaila opened her door and saw Echo gnawing on his bone, of course on her bed.

"Echo, off! You know better."

Echo barked a couple of times before dragging his bone to the edge and dropping it off. He then leapt at Kaila, his tail wagging a mile a minute.

"Fine. I can't stay mad at you." She spent a few minutes playing with him before throwing her clothes in the growing pile on the floor and grabbed a pair of sweats and a t-shirt.

"So how's the food?" Kaila asked, a smile on her face.

"It was great, I love your mom's cooking," Holly said with a grin, rubbing her stomach. "What are you doing today?"

"I was going to take out Echo and then no idea."

"Do you want to go to the movies with us?"

"I'd just be a third wheel," Kaila said, flopping into the chair.

"Why don't you invite what's his name?"

"You mean Sam?"

"Yeah. See if he wants to come. Maybe we can go out for supper first."

"Sure. That sounds like fun. I'll text him and see if he's free." Kaila left to find her phone. She grabbed her purse off the bed and rummaged through to the bottom, but no phone. *What the heck, where did it go?* Kaila looked around the floor, hoping to see it. With a sigh she slid to the ground on her knees and crawled around, peering under the bed. Echo watched her from his bed for a minute before deciding it must be a game and bounded out trying to jump on her back.

"Echo, stop! You better not have dragged my phone somewhere." He stopped and gave his 'I have no idea what you're talking about' look before leaving the room. Kaila groaned and began lifting the clothes, shaking them before beginning a new pile. *I guess I'm doing laundry today.* Kaila lifted her phone up in triumph. Her fingers flew over the keys and she was back in the kitchen grabbing her plate in no time.

With her plate piled high, she trooped to the living room to stare at the television.

"I'm not sure if we need to go out for supper after this," Holly commented. Both Brian and Kaila looked at her in shock.

"What! Not have supper, are you nuts?" Kaila demanded.

Holly glanced from the T.V. "Sorry, I forgot who I was talking to." She laughed.

"I would think so," Kaila muttered as Brian tried to hold back his grin.

Kaila licked her fingers as she put her plate in the sink and felt a buzz. "It's a date!" she hollered.

"Good, where do you want to eat?" Holly asked.

"How about Swiss Chalet, I haven't been there for a while. Something light will be good so I have room for my popcorn."

Holly rolled her eyes as she shook her head in agreement. "What time?"

"Why don't we go at 4:30, which would give me time to do laundry?" Kaila said, looking at the clock.

"That would work. We have some shopping to do, so why don't we meet you guys there?"

"Sure. And I'll clean up, don't worry about it." Kaila said, shooing Holly and Brian out of the kitchen.

"You're sure?" Brian asked.

"Yeah, I'm here anyways."

Kaila shoved her clothes into the basket, but as she reached for the last shirt, Echo ran in, grabbed it and ran out.

"Son of a..." Kaila cried as she dropped the basket, running after him.

"Dammit, Echo. What is with you today? I know you want out. We'll go when I'm done with the clothes. So you have to give me that shirt."

She watched as he dropped his butt and growled while shaking her shirt back and forth, his ears

152

following the same path. Kaila stomped over, picked up his wiggling form and headed towards his dog carrier. His body tensed and he seemed to know what the outcome was going to be and his squirming intensified.

"No! I need to get some work done before we go out. So you're going to have to stay in here." Kaila pulled her now hole-ridden shirt out of his mouth and quickly pushed him into the carrier, closing the door before he could escape. She could hear his whimpering and scratching as she entered her room. Kaila glared at the offending shirt a moment before throwing it in the garbage can and picking up her basket. *At least it wasn't one of my favorites.*

Thankfully, the laundry room was empty and Kaila opened a lid, dumping the clothes. She grabbed the soap, poured in a capful and pushed the button. *Crap!* Nothing happened. Kaila kicked the machine and did a little hop as her toe bent backwards. She hobbled to the other machine and lifted the lid. *Arrgh.* Brightly colored clothes stared back at her. This day was just not going right. She yanked her clothes out of the washer into the basket and stomped back to their apartment.

Kaila was slamming the dishes into the cupboard when the phone rang. Taking a deep breath, Kaila slowly reached over and picked up the phone.

"Hey, Kaila."

"Hi, Sam. What's up?"

"Do you want me to come over earlier? Maybe we can have a couple of drinks."

"Sorry. I have some chores to finish before we go out."

"How about I bring some wine and help you?"

Kaila could feel herself wavering. "Sure, why not. I could use the company."

"OK, I'll see you in a bit."

Kaila felt a little giddy as she hung up.

By the time Sam knocked on the door, Kaila had been able to get one load of laundry done, the dishes washed and was just finishing cleaning the kitchen.

"Hey, Kaila, I come bearing gifts." Sam stood in the hall with a large grin and a twinkle in his eye, holding a bottle.

"Come in, come in." Kaila grabbed him by the sleeve, dragging his body through the door and slamming it behind. Before he could get another word out, she pulled his body close and pressed her lips to his. She saw the shock in his face before closing her eyes and letting herself go.

Finally pulling away, Kaila gave him a large grin as she grabbed the bottle of wine.

"Glad you could come," Kaila said.

"So am I." Sam stood at the kitchen entrance watching her with a bemused expression. Kaila searched for the opener and smiled in triumph after she pulled it out of the drawer.

"Would you like to open while I grab glasses?" Kaila asked.

"Sure."

"So, what's first?" Sam asked as he sipped the wine.

"I have clothes to fold and need to tidy up in the living room."

"Well, let's get at it. Where's Echo?"

"He's in the kennel."

"Oh, oh, been naughty, has he?"

Kaila laughed before saying, "Yes, he ripped one of my shirts and kept getting in the way."

They worked comfortably together as Kaila folded clothes on the couch and Sam cleaned the room. Finishing the last shirt, she stood up and stretched before carrying the basket back to her room. She didn't realize Sam had followed until Kaila heard the bedroom door close and he spun her around. He enclosed his arms around her and dipped his head down to capture her lips in a searing kiss. Kaila wrapped her arms around his neck and pulled him closer. Before she knew it, they were hurriedly unbuttoning each other's shirts, their breath coming out quickly.

"We don't have much time," Kaila said.

"I'll make the most of it," Sam said as he grabbed her again for another soul-searing kiss.

"We have to hurry," Kaila said, looking at the clock as she grabbed clothes from the closet.

"What time are we meeting them?"

"4:30."

"That's in half an hour. You better move it," Sam said, watching her rifle through the closet again.

"Just get out so I can get ready." Kaila laughed, pushing Sam out the door. "Don't forgot this." She shoved his shirt against his well-honed chest and closed the door. She could hear him laughing on the other side as she pulled on her jeans.

Ten minutes later, they were walking out of the apartment. "I'm really going to have to take Echo out tomorrow before he goes nuts," Kaila said.

Holly and Brian were already seated when they arrived. Brian stood up and shook hands with Sam as Kaila slid into the booth.

"Hi, guys," Kaila said breathlessly.

"How was your afternoon? Did you get much accomplished?" Holly asked.

Kaila felt her face heat up as she answered, "Well the apartment is cleaned. And one of the stupid washers is broken."

"I think your room's a mess again." Sam grinned. Kaila elbowed him to shut up, just as the waitress arrived. "Saved by the bell," he said.

Kaila glared at him before turning to ask for a drink. She could see Holly and Brian were trying to hide their grins, and her face felt even hotter.

"So, what movie are we going to see?" Kaila asked, trying to change the subject.

"How about we see the second *Hunger Games?*" Holly suggested.

Both men groaned in denial and Kaila offered, "How about *Thor II?*"

"I second that!" Brian said with a smile. "Come on, Holly. You know you want to."

"I guess." Holly sighed, knowing she was outnumbered.

"OK, where are we going to sit?" Kaila whispered, peering into the darkened theatre. The movie was going to start right away; traffic had been horrendous. It was a good thing *Thor II* was not a new release, or there wouldn't be any seats.

"Over there." Sam nudged the girls up the steps towards the top. *At least it isn't right in the front; that would have sucked,* Kaila thought. She had seen *Avatar* in 3D in the third row. Now that had bit the big one.

They all got seated and passed treats around just as the opening credits began. Sam leaned over and whispered in Kaila's ear, "Do you want to do something after the movie?"

"No, I better get some sleep. I'm going to be busy with this case tomorrow. A rain check?" Kaila asked with a smile.

"No problem."

Chapter 17

"George, how was your weekend?" Kaila asked.

"Nothing special. You sure seem chipper."

"I got some rest yesterday. I didn't think about the case for most of the day."

"That's good. Maybe you have a fresh perspective."

"I did come in Saturday to look over our notes to see if we missed anything."

"And?"

"Nothing. I think we're on the right track with the parents."

"I agree. The lawsuits were a dead end. We should check into Mr. and Mrs. Walkers' finances. See if there is anything suspicious there. We'll also need to start looking at Mr. Bates's background. I wonder if Rachel's parents are back yet."

"Let's try them first before we begin digging more."

"How about you gather all our information and I'll figure out our questions we're going to grill them with. Then we can head out. It's too early for them, anyways."

Kaila typed in John Bates into the computer and waited for the results. She already knew he was a realtor, but she was looking to see what else he was into. It didn't take long for the information to pop up. There was his web page, which didn't hold any secrets. There were also quite a few John Bates in the world. A baseball player, an actor and comic character....who knew. Kaila was finishing up her search when there was a tap on her shoulder.

"Ready to go?"

"Sure, there's nothing else to find."

Light flakes were falling as the sun shone. Kaila didn't understand how that was possible; it was a common occurrence during rainstorms as well.

After maneuvering out of the parking lot, George asked, "What excitement did you get into this weekend?"

"Not a whole lot."

"Come on, I have to live vicariously through you."

"Fine, but what about your daughter?" Kaila laughed.

"You really think I want to know the things my daughter is doing? You want me to have a heart attack?" he demanded.

"I guess not." Kaila smiled. "I saw my folks on Friday and had a good home-cooked meal. Came to the station for a bit and a couple of us went and saw *Thor II.* It was a good movie."

"Was it with Sam?" George asked slyly.

"If you must know, yes. Also Holly and Brian," Kaila said primly, trying to hide her grin.

"Young love, there's nothing like it," George said, sighing. Kaila just gave an unladylike snort.

"So, did you call the Walkers?" Kala asked.

"No, I thought showing up would be better. Harder for the housekeeper to get rid of us."

"Good thinking. Do you think they're back?"

"Well, it's been a week; depending on why they left, maybe."

George knocked sharply on the Walkers' door.

"Yes?" the housekeeper asked as she opened the door. "Oh, it's you. Do you have any information?"

"Is Mr. and Mrs. Walker back?"

"They just arrived; let me check if they'll see you."

"I would think they—" Before Kaila could finish, the housekeeper had shut the door.

"What the heck!" George growled.

A few minutes later, the door opened and Mr. Walker stood in front of them.

"Have you found my girl's killer?" he demanded.

"Can we come in for a few minutes? We have some questions," George requested through clenched teeth. Kaila felt the same. After disappearing during the investigation, not letting the police know, he had the gall to ask in that tone?

"OK. But please make it quick. We just got home and we're exhausted."

They followed him into the living room and sat on the couch he indicated.

"Will Mrs. Walker be joining us?" Kaila asked.

"No. She's resting."

"We would like to ask her some questions," Kaila insisted.

"If it could wait until another day...so, what can I help you with?"

Kaila looked over at George and raised her brow. *What the heck was going on?*

"Can we ask why you left town?" George questioned.

Mr. Walker looked surprised as he said, "Didn't our housekeeper tell you we went on vacation?"

159

"Yes. But why did you leave during the investigation?" George asked.

"We had this planned for a while and would have lost our money. And Jackie needed to get away from all this, all the calls," Mr. Walker said, waving his hand.

"Calls from who?" Kaila asked.

"Lots of people were calling about Rachel, friends and reporters. What have you found out?"

"We haven't discovered a motive. There seems to be nothing in her personal life or work. We tracked down her boyfriend—"

"Boyfriend! She didn't have one."

"Didn't Mrs. Walker tell you? We talked to her before your trip. Anyways, he didn't know what happened."

"So, it could have been a random attack?" he asked. To Kaila it sounded like relief in his voice.

"We're not sure, but it's a coincidence that Victoria was murdered as well."

"What! When did this happen?" Mr. Walker demanded.

"You haven't been in contact with Mr. Bates?" George asked.

"No." Mr. Walker crumbled into the chair and put his head into his hands. "Why is this happening?" he moaned.

"If you would have stayed in contact while on your vacation, this wouldn't be a shock. We need to know if you or Mrs. Walker had any problems at work or in your personal relationships," Kaila said, a little snidely.

"No. Nothing. What could we have done that was so bad to warrant killing our daughter?"

"We're not sure. There've been no calls or emails?"

"No."

"What about money? Do you owe anyone?"

It took him a minute to answer. "No. We have plenty of money, why would I need to borrow money?"

"We just need to check every angle, Mr. Walker."

"Do you know if anyone has been bothering Mrs. Walker?" Kaila asked.

"No, she would have told me."

"That was a bold move asking to see their computer and finances. You got us kicked out," Kaila said as the door was slammed shut in their faces, which was becoming a habit for them.

"We weren't going to get anything else, and it was worth a try. Well, on to Mr. Bates."

"Good thing we're close, maybe we'll beat Mr. Walker before he calls."

"Why do you think that?"

"There has to be something going on that they're not telling, and with their daughters being best friends and attending the same club.... Also, he just got into town and found out about Victoria. He didn't look happy when you asked those questions; he seemed real nervous."

"Never thought of that. Let's move it."

They pulled up a few seconds later and rushed to the door.

"So he's here?" Kaila asked.

"Yeah, I called him before we left the station."

Kaila knocked on the door and tried to peek through the side window. She saw Mr. Bates walking towards them, the phone to his ear.

"Crap, we're too late."

"I'll have to call you later," Mr. Bates said as he opened the door.

Kaila could hear a man's voice, she was sure it was Mr. Walker, saying "wait—"

Mr. Bates hung up. "Come in. So, what did you find out?"

"Not a lot. We need to ask you some questions about your life," Kaila answered, and a look of surprise crossed his face.

"Why?"

"Maybe there's someone upset with you?" George suggested.

"No!"

"There's no one that's furious with you. Threatening messages? Maybe a house-deal gone south?" Kaila questioned.

"Nothing like that. Of course there are unsatisfied buyers and sellers, but not enough to kill."

"They never sent you an angry email or text, even if you didn't take it seriously?" George asked.

"No, No!"

"Would you mind if we took a look at your email? Maybe there's something there that you would overlook? The tech is already checking out Victoria's and since the laptop is already in the lab—" George snuck a quick glance at Kaila as he asked. She slowly shook her head.

"I don't think so. I have confidential documents on there."

"Mr. Bates, what about your club?" Kaila interjected.

"What about it?"

"Is there anyone from there that would have a grudge?"

Mr. Bates thought for a second. "I can't imagine anyone like that. I think you're on the wrong track," he said, shaking his head.

"We need to follow up on every angle, Mr. Bates. We'll need to talk with your coworkers and friends. Maybe they know something," George said.

Mr. Bates groaned and closed his eyes. "Do you have to? I don't want you bugging people."

"Do you want us to find your daughter's killer? We need to continue investigating everything we can."

"Fine. Fine. Just please be discreet. Now, if you could leave, I need to meet some clients."

"Thanks for your time. We'll keep you informed," Kaila said.

"OK, what now?" Kaila asked, climbing into the truck.

"Let's head back to the station, write all this up and then maybe we can begin questioning their coworkers."

"So, do you know what's going on?" Kaila asked.

"I think there's something suspicious, but for the life of me, I can't figure it out. The common thread is the club and the girls. And it's too much a coincidence for it to be a random sequence of murders."

"I agree. We just have to keep at it and hopefully something turns up before anyone else is hurt."

Chapter 18

He tapped his fingers on the steering wheel as he glared out the snow-encrusted window. What the hell was he doing now? He had been wasting all day following this kid around, waiting for the right opportunity. How trivial were the rich, nothing to worry about except where to have the next party and who to screw over. The boy eventually left the store and swaggered towards his car, stopping to ogle a gorgeous woman walking by. As if that kid had a chance. The man pulled out into traffic a couple cars behind him and continued to tail the target. The man was beginning to panic; when could he do it? *Maybe nighttime was better; of course it was, stupid!* He needed to calm down and think. It was a weeknight, but the kid was young and stupid. He would be going out tonight like every other. Hopefully he had a chance then. The period of time for this project wasn't long. He had another person to see after, someone close to his heart.

The boy stumbled out of the club, laughing and waving off his friends.

Stupid, stupid, he shouldn't be driving. The man grabbed the gun out of the glove compartment and slowly opened his door. He made his way to the alley and lurked in the shadows, waiting for his victim to appear. It wasn't long before he could hear a stumble, a crash, and the cursing began. He felt a giggle rise and clamped his hand onto his mouth, trying to keep any sound from escaping.

As the shadow walked by, the man stepped out and pushed the gun into the kid's side.

"Don't say anything or I'll blow your brains out!"

The boy looked surprised and scared while he tried to turn and run.

"Huh, huh, you're not going anywhere." The man grabbed the kid's arm in a tight grip and steered him towards the waiting vehicle.

"What do you think you're doing?" the boy snarled.

"I'm kidnapping you, what does it look like?"

"Do you know who I am?"

"Of course, Gerald Radcliff." The man enjoyed the look of shock that crossed Gerald's face.

"Well, then, you know my parents can pay you. You look familiar, don't I know you?" Gerald's voice reached a high pitch as he was dragged forward.

"Why do you think I want money?" The man glanced around the deserted streets before popping the trunk. Seeing this, Gerald opened his mouth, but received a blow from the gun to his head, dropping him to the ground before he could make a sound.

Man, it's a good thing this kid was drunk. Quickly grabbing the rope from within, he bound up Gerald's arms and legs, and covered his mouth before grunting and heaving him into the trunk and slamming it shut. It must be a sign that no one had spotted them yet. There was approval for his cause and that made him smile and hum as he hurried to the door and jumped in.

He had only been driving for half an hour when banging and screaming could be heard faintly through the metal. Damn, he had hoped the kid would stay knocked out until he could be moved to the cabin. They eventually pulled up and he slowly climbed out, worrying what he should do next. The man needed some tools; that would be the smart thing to do. Never underestimate the enemy. It took him a few minutes of rummaging in the shed before coming out carrying a crow bar. He pushed the button and stood to the side as he slowly lifted the lid. Two bound feet shoved through the opening, looking for contact, but finding nothing. Instead, there was a large crack as the bar connected with bone and a muffled scream of agony.

"You thought you were smarter than me; in what universe? You're nothing and I'm the one that will shatter your world. Don't even think of fighting back or you'll feel more pain."

He peered into the darkness, his weapon at the ready. What met his searching eyes was a scared little boy; that gave him some pleasure, seeing that. He deserved everything he was going to get. His father shouldn't have done that; shouldn't have taken everything away.

The man made a threatening gesture before laying down the bar and pulling him out. Before they got far, the kid passed out and the man had to drag him the rest of the way. Gerald's head banged on the steps as they made their way painfully towards the door. The man could feel sweat soaking his shirt and cursed the kid; he shouldn't have to do all this work. After slamming the door shut behind them, he pulled and dragged the body to the chair, where he tied Gerald up nice and tight. No one was going to escape tonight.

167

The man threw a cupful of water into Gerald's face and then stepped back waiting for him to finish sputtering.

"You finished?"

All Gerald could do was growl and scream through the rag. "I can't remove that, it's too risky. You're not like the girls." The man could see the terror and understanding enter Gerald's eyes and couldn't help the little thrill running up his back.

"I know you have questions, but we really don't have time for them. We have to hurry before we're discovered." Gerald began to thrash and buck against the chair. The man swore as he cuffed Gerald on the side of the head, stopping him for the moment.

"Enough of that!" he snarled. "I'm sorry, but you had this coming and the more you struggle, the worse the pain will be. If you'd just accept the inevitable, it will go quickly." Gerald shook his head in denial and tried to move. The man began pulling out his tools and caressed them a moment before putting them down in front of Gerald.

Gerald's eyes widened as he stared at the horror in front of him. "I had a chance to use these on your friends; do you want to hear how they screamed and begged for their lives?" He giggled as Gerald began to push his feet against the floor and almost toppled over backwards.

"OK, that's enough! You've gone and made me mad." He reached down and grabbed a large knife. "Hush little baby, don't say a word, Papa's gonna buy you a mockingbird, if that mockingbird don't sing, Papa's gonna buy you a diamond ring...." He continued singing as the knife moved up and down, occasionally sticking into the body. Soon, the thrashing stopped and the man looked down at the carnage. He wasn't sorry, not like with the girls. Maybe he was becoming numb to the killing. There was so much blood, a lot more than

168

before. That made him angry all over again and he was glad that Gerald was dead; he deserved it. He pulled off his gloves and threw them on the bags.

As he scrubbed the floors, the man debated on where he should throw the body: he wanted to send a message. He needed to destroy his enemies, but dumping at the park might be too dangerous now. He needed to think; there was time. The voices cheered, making him smile again and he scrubbed harder.

Chapter 19

"Hi, Holly, how's it going?" Kaila asked, walking into the apartment.

"Fine. You don't look too good. Is the case getting to you?"

"Yes. I'm not sure where to look now. We didn't have much luck with the parents' coworkers, though there are still a few to interview tomorrow. But I don't think we're going to get anywhere."

"You found nothing from the girls' backgrounds?"

"No. This really sucks. I'm worried something worse is going to happen. How's your job and school going?"

"Very busy. There's a backlog sitting in the coolers, and school is exhausting. I can't afford to stay as long as necessary to help make a dent."

"At least you're not bored." Kaila smiled. "What are you doing tonight?"

"I'm sitting here watching T.V. Then I'll drag my ass to bed when my eyes start to close."

"That sounds like a plan. I think I'll join you. So, are you going home anytime soon?"

"I don't know. Mom is coming in Saturday for lunch and shopping."

"That'll be nice. What does she think of Brian?"

"She really likes him," Holly said with a grin. "I think she's hoping for grandchildren soon."

Kaila laughed. "How many kids does she have you popping out?"

"They're not popcorn," Holly said, poking Kaila's arm. "And I think it's at least two."

"I think you'll make a great mom."

"Thanks, you too."

"Maybe, eventually. But I'm not like you, Holly. I don't have those urges right now."

"Give it time, Kaila, you're still young."

"OK, enough serious talk. What are we watching?"

"I think there's a marathon of *The Big Bang Theory.*"

"That sounds good. I need a few laughs." Kaila grabbed a pillow and sank into the chair. "Tomorrow's another day."

"So, are you ready to roll?" Kaila asked, throwing her purse on the desk.

"You seem chipper," George commented.

"Because I did nothing last night."

"Well, hopefully you're fully charged. We have a full day of questioning."

"Should we maybe go back to the club? The girls were our focus last time."

"We'll go later. Nighttime should be a better time to catch Mr. Walker and Mr. Bates's friends."

"Do you have everything we—"

"Hey, you two," a cop said breathlessly as he ran up.

"What?" George asked.

"They found another body."

"Who is it?" Kaila asked as a feeling of dread passed over her.

"They said his name was Gerald."

"Gerald Radcliff?" George asked, standing up.

"I think so. Wasn't he someone you were questioning before?"

"Yes. Where's the body?" George demanded, grabbing his jacket.

"It's in the south end of Glenmore Park in the river."

"Crap!" Kaila exclaimed as she followed George out. *Would this nightmare ever end? What was the purpose of the killings? They had to be by the same person.*

They trudged to the crime scene and came to an abrupt halt. Detectives were milling around and some tried keeping the crowd back as the others investigated the scene.

"Damn, Kaila, what's going on?" George muttered, pulling out a smoke.

"I'm not sure, but we'd better figure it out. And soon."

George inhaled quickly and then threw the smoke to the ground, crushed it with his toe and headed down the slope. It was slow going as they slid down the slope, trying to find a grip for their toes in the wet embankment.

"So, what do we have?" George asked the detective standing at the water bank.

"The victim was found along the bank. His body was wedged in the tree roots over there." The detective pointed to the left.

Kaila and George gingerly stepped down the bank through the snow, trying not to trip over the stumps and limbs littering the ground. George pushed back the branches along the path and asked, "How do you think someone found the body? It wasn't visible from the path, right?"

"No idea. Maybe Gerald was wearing something bright, something that reflected the sun."

"There has to be a common thread between these kids and we need to find it now," George said as he slipped on a patch of ice. Kaila grabbed his arm and kept him steady and he flashed her a grateful smile.

"I have to be careful, a fall like that could break the hip of someone as old as myself."

Kaila started laughing, "Give me a break. You're not old."

"You haven't seen me trying to get out of bed." George grinned.

"And I don't want to." Kaila came to an abrupt halt as the bloated body of Gerald Radcliff came into view. She covered her mouth quickly and turned away, trying to steady her breathing.

"It looks like he's escalating," George said, putting a hand on Kaila's shoulder.

Kaila took a couple more breaths and gave George a weak smile as she walked slowly toward the detectives.

As they drew near, Kaila could see the torture Gerald must have endured. His hands were taped behind his back and there were stab wounds all over his chest and arms. Because of his journey down river, there were also scratch marks and scrapes from what looked like tree branches and probably rocks along the riverbank. She could also see what looked like bite marks across his exposed torso. Kaila glanced towards the partially ice-covered river. The detectives had broken the ice at the bank in order to drag Gerald's body out, not that the ice was that thick yet.

"How many more are there going to be?" Kaila whispered as they were approached by a detective.

"Can I see your badge?"

George pulled out his before saying, "The victim was part of our investigation in two other murders."

"That's a tough break."

"How was he found way off the path?" Kaila questioned, looking back from where they had come. She could just see the hats of the detectives patrolling the crime scene. It wasn't possible.

"I guess he was lucky someone walking their dog came by. The dog got loose and ran down here."

Kaila felt shivers up her spine. *Had that person been at risk like me and Echo? The killer could have been watching either of them from a distance.* Kaila gave a little shake and asked, "Where's the witness?"

"We interviewed him and sent them home."

"Have you found anything yet?" George asked.

"No. We think he was dumped further up the river; there were no prints here. Nothing seems to be disturbed except for what the witness and his dog touched."

"If he wasn't dropped here, I wonder if the killer planned for us to find the body. The girls were in a much more public, accessible place. Does it look like he's been in the water long?" Kaila commented.

"I don't think it's been long, but we'll have to wait and see what the autopsy shows."

The detective walked away and Kaila just stood staring at the body. There were all kinds of psychos out there, but who would want to kill a bunch of kids? They weren't old enough, hopefully, to piss anyone off that much.

There was thrashing and cursing from behind and Kaila spun around to see a gurney appear between the trees and the paramedics following behind.

"Hi, guys," George said, as he and Kaila jumped out of their way.

175

"So, now what? Do we want to talk to his parents first or continue onto the other parents' work?" Kaila asked.

"We better see Gerald's parents before they find out about the murder another way."

They trudged back up the hill and Kaila stopped a minute, looking back to watch them lift Gerald into a bag and plop him onto the stretcher.

Chapter 20

He wished it had been possible to see the action. Discovering the body and seeing the devastation would have been exciting, for him anyways. But it was too dangerous; he couldn't be discovered. There was still more to do. The voices were getting stronger and more insistent. Maybe once he completed the last task, they would be silent.

       The man sat at the single chair in the kitchen, staring at his hands. They were becoming stained with blood, no matter how much he scrubbed. It reminded him of the story Shakespeare wrote about the woman who kept scrubbing her hands after killing; couldn't remember what the story was though. It didn't matter. At the start, he never imagined this would be the outcome, but there was no turning back now. He had done some evil but necessary things. The police, of course, wouldn't see it like that. It was black and white for them, justice didn't come into the picture.

       He tried to think of something pleasant. A small smile splayed across his face as he pictured his boy and girl running to him with open arms. They were his life, the reason to live. He snarled as his ex came into the picture and the mental image dissipated like it was never there. He pushed his chair away with such force, it flew across the room and hit the wall.

He stomped to the living room and faced the table covered in papers. Pulling out the ring from his pocket, he placed it on the table beside the pair of glasses and the crushed pink phone. Soon it would be over and he'd have his prize, his revenge.

Chapter 21

"I hope I never get used to this," Kaila muttered, standing behind George on the Radcliff porch.

George nodded in agreement as he rang the bell. Not that anyone really deserved killing, but—it was sure as hell easier to swallow a drug dealer being murdered as opposed to a youth.

"Hello, can I help you?" The woman standing in front of them was older, probably in her mid-sixties. Her hair was short, brown with white streaks, and she was wearing a rather tight shirt and pants that weren't quite suitable to her body type.

"Hello, are you Mrs. Radcliff?" George asked, holding out his badge.

"Yes. What do you want?" she asked, with suspicion in her eyes.

"Can we come in?" Kaila inquired.

Mrs. Radcliff stood for a moment staring at them before opening the door and beckoning them in. "Come this way." She led them to a small sitting room off the foyer. "So, what's this about?"

"Is Mr. Radcliff in?" George inquired.

"No. He's at the office."

"Well, there's no way to say this...I'm sorry, Mrs. Radcliff, but Gerald has been killed," Kaila said quietly.

"No!" Mrs. Radcliff wailed. "It can't be him, I just saw him...it's your fault!" she pointed an accusative finger in their direction. "You were talking with him last week. What did you do?" Mrs. Radcliff demanded.

"We were asking him questions about his friends' murders. He wasn't in trouble," Kaila answered.

"I want you to leave, I have to call my husband," she said, standing up.

"We just have to ask you a few questions," George said.

"Not right now. You will have to come back." With that, she stalked to the door and swung it open, staring in their direction until they followed.

"We'll call you later, Mrs. Radcliff, about coming over," Kaila informed.

"You do that." And the door shut with a loud bang.

"What is going on with these people?" George demanded. "Don't any of them care about their kids?"

"Let's head back to the station and talk to the captain. I think we're going to need more men. And I'm sure we'll get DNA back linking the murderer to the girls."

"Yeah, let's get out of here. There's lots we're going to have to do."

They hurried to the truck amid a flurry of snowflakes. It was starting to come down thick. "Hopefully they are finished at the crime scene," Kaila said, slamming the door.

"Hey, Captain, do you have a minute?" George called as they ran into the station.

The captain waved them in and Kaila flopped into a chair.

"We need more men," George stated.

"What's happening?"

"Gerald Radcliff was just killed. We interviewed him in our investigation for our two vics. He was a friend of theirs. A pedestrian just found his body in the river."

"How far have you gotten in your investigation?"

"We were just starting on the girls' parents. So far, nothing concrete has come out. And now the weather has decided to not cooperate. I'm not sure how far they got on the crime scene."

"OK, we'll meet in the conference room in twenty. I'll find some other detectives to draft. Gather all the information so you can brief the rest. Now out," the captain said and walked closely out on their heels.

"So, you want to do the talking?" Kaila asked.

"Sure. But make sure you speak up if I miss anything."

The twenty minutes flew by as they hurriedly gathered everything they could on the cases. It was urgent that the investigation had a jumpstart. They could be looking at a serial killer. How many more were going to be targeted? Was it going to end at three? All these questions were running through Kaila's head as they rushed to the meeting.

There were four other detectives along with the captain waiting for Kaila and George. The room went silent as all eyes turned to them. *Great!* Kaila thought. One of the detectives was her biggest fan. He was old school and had voiced his concerns to their captain numerous times about women in the police force. Her first experience involving him had been as a constable. It was a gruesome domestic violence call where she and her partner were first on the scene. Kaila was checking the vitals on the wife's mangled body while her partner arrested the husband. Everything was going fine until the detective arrived and saw Kaila leaning over the body. Man did the shit hit the fan. What was she doing? The scene was contaminated now. On and on he went until the ambulance arrived and pushed him out of the way. It didn't matter that the paramedics agreed Kaila had followed the right steps. Since then, Kaila winced every time she saw him. And, of course, she was sure that immediately after seeing her walk into the squad room he ran to the captain's office.

George cleared his throat as Kaila sat down.

"We have three bodies. The first two happened a week ago. They were best friends and found three days apart. The third was found this morning. His name is Gerald and he knew both girls. All three families are members at the same exclusive club and the kids went to the same high school. We have checked the background of both girls. The only hiccup was a girl named Delia who harassed Victoria in high school and partied with the girls the weekend before. The first victim, Rachel, her parents disappeared for a week's vacation soon after the murder."

There were looks of surprise around the room and one of the detectives raised his hand. "What was their reason, did they really go vacationing or was it work?"

"They swear it was booked before and it was a vacation," George answered.

"So, we need to split up the families and recheck backgrounds, interview family and friends. If you two will talk with Rachel's side and you guys can take Victoria's, the second victim. Kaila and I will deal with Gerald's parents. All the notes are on the computer for you to access and we'll meet at the end of each day to compare notes. We'll see how far everyone gets and whomever is done first can go back to the club. Alright, everyone, let's get out of here."

The captain nodded his head in agreement as he walked by. "Keep me in the loop."

"You got it," George said.

The detectives finished asking their questions and left to start their investigations.

Kaila sipped the Coke plopped in front of her by the waitress as George fiddled with his notebook, staring at his scribbles.

"I don't know how you can read that," Kaila said.

George grinned, "I could have been a doctor with this."

"Do you think we'll find something with Gerald's parents?" Kaila asked.

"Someone has to know something," George said with frustration. "I could see maybe someone being pissed at Gerald, but not to kill the girls as well. Gerald seems to be the type to have shady friends."

"It'll be interesting, I'm sure the other families have already called the Radcliffs'."

"I'm sure they have. It seems like they're circling the wagons. I'm ready, let's get this over with," George said, pulling on his jacket.

Kaila grimaced.

"You're sure they're expecting us? What did they say when you called?" George demanded as he pounded on the door.

"Yes. They're both home." The door crashed open and a large, grim man stood before them.

"I'm coming, you don't need to knock the door down!"

"Sorry, sir. Can we come in? We're Detectives Porter and Hapner. I called you earlier."

"Yes, come in."

"We're sorry for your loss, Mr. Radcliff," George said.

"Thank you. What you would you like to know?"

"When's the last time you saw your son?" Kaila asked.

"He went out with friends last night. We don't really keep track of him. He's a grown boy," Mr. Radcliff answered.

"Did you notice what time he left? It'll give us a starting point," Kaila asked.

Mr. Radcliff looked at his wife before saying, "He was here for supper at five. After that, I'm not sure when he left. I was busy in the study."

Kaila looked over at Mrs. Radcliff and waited.

"I'm not sure either." She sniffed and took a deep breath. "I was reading in our room. I think I heard the door open around six-thirty."

"How good of friends was he with Rachel and Victoria?"

"We saw them at the club and he was a couple of years ahead of them in school. But, otherwise, I don't know," Mrs. Radcliff said.

"We'll need a list of his friends," George stated.

She nodded and stood up.

"Can you think of anyone who would want to hurt him? Was he being harassed?" Kaila asked.

"No, though I'm not sure if he would have told us. The last couple of years we didn't talk a lot," Mr. Radcliff answered.

"Can we look at his computer and phone?"

"I guess. Harriet!"

"Yes?" she said, peeking her head around the corner.

"Grab Gerald's computer, and his phone, if it's there."

She quickly disappeared and Kaila heard stomping above them.

"Did you find Gerald's car? It's not here."

"What kind of car did he have?" Kaila asked.

"He drove a BMW."

I wish, Kaila thought to herself.

"We'll look for it and let you know."

"What about either you or Mrs. Radcliff, any problems with anyone?"

"I, of course, get clients upset when they lose money, but that's sometimes a consequence to playing the stock market. They should all know the risks. I ensure everything is laid out on the table before I continue. I don't think anyone's that angry."

Kaila stared at his face while he gave his spiel. She watched as his eyes shifted up and down and he grimaced slightly.

"Is there someone you thought of?" Kaila asked.

"No, no. Just thinking about my son," he denied, shaking his head.

"I've got them," Mrs. Radcliff said, stepping into the room. "But I didn't see his phone."

"Didn't think it'd be there, he never left without it. I think him and his friends text each other while sitting at the same table."

"Thanks," George said, standing up and taking the computer and paper. "We'll start with Gerald's friends and try to retrace his steps. You need to come and confirm the body," George said.

"But didn't you already? I don't think I can," Mrs. Radcliff cried.

"No, we need a family member to identify the body."

"I can't. No! No!"

Mr. Radcliff rushed over to Harriet and held her close.

"Please leave. Keep us informed. I want this bastard caught," he demanded. "Doesn't seem like you've done much, so far," he muttered under his breath.

Kaila shifted her eyes to see if George would respond. Hopefully not; they didn't need that. With a silent thanks, Kaila watched George continue towards the door.

"Thanks for your cooperation," Kaila said. "We'll be in touch."

Kaila and George quickly exited the house, closing the door quietly behind them.

"They're more cooperative than the other two parents," George commented, gingerly walking down the steps.

"They're not what I expected. So, off to the station?" Kaila asked, looking at the papers in his hands.

"Yep. We have a place to start," George said. "Let's get this to IT and make some calls to his friends. Hopefully something will break."

"Sounds good. We need to keep an eye out for his car. Maybe the car is at the crime scene."

Kaila was elected to descend into the dungeon again. She found the same tech hard at work.

"No music this time?" Kaila asked, laughing.

"Haha." He looked up. "I knew you were coming. What do you have?"

"This is the latest victim's laptop. Can you work your magic? We need to know what he's been up to and if anything has been deleted."

"No problem. Put it on the pile." He pointed to the desk covered with other laptops and electronics.

"Is there any way you can look at it now?"

"You want to jump the queue?" He frowned in her direction.

"Please. It's looking like there might be a serial killer out there." Kaila tried to look sad, which wasn't too difficult if she pictured the victims.

"Fine, fine. Give it here. I probably won't get back to you till tomorrow though," he warned.

"That's fine. You're a lifesaver. Thanks," Kaila said with a grin, handing over the computer.

She hurried upstairs before the tech could change his mind.

"He's going to look at it today!" Kaila said, looking over George's shoulder.

"Great! How did you swing that?"

"I begged. I'm not above that, especially if it helps a case."

"Good girl. I'm just going through the list of Gerald's friends. Here, you take the bottom half," George said, ripping the paper and handing over Kaila's share.

"Have you talked to any of them yet?"

"No. I'm doing research for ammunition first. These kids nowadays don't want to give anything up."

"Now that's the truth."

Kaila looked over the list she was holding. There were seven guys and two girls. Sometimes you had to be careful. She'd been caught by surprise a few times with a suspect's name. Kaila laughed to herself as she pictured Marian. Kaila's reaction had been priceless. On one of her first cases with George, a dancer had been killed at a nightclub and they were investigating one of her coworkers. It turned out Marian was a male crossdresser; Kaila didn't have experience with the transgender society. Once they left the club, George had split a gut. She had thought he was going to hurt himself. At least he kept his word about not letting anyone at the station know. Kaila faced enough razzing without that coming to light.

Kaila faced her computer and began the tedious job of research. Nothing exciting came up about the girls, but a couple of the boys were in the system for some petty crimes, like shoplifting.

I wonder if Gerald had graduated to bigger and better things. He didn't have an arrest record.

"Hey, George, what kind of friends are you looking into?"

"What do you mean?" George asked, looking up.

"Well, I've got a couple of petty thieves here."

"So far these are squeaky clean. I wonder if Gerald got himself into a bind."

"I'm curious what Gerald's computer will show. Was there something that he was into that got him killed?" Kaila wondered out loud.

"Maybe his death isn't related to the girls at all," George said, shaking his head. "But I can't shake the feeling that's not the case."

"Me neither. Let's finish this up and start visiting his friends. Hopefully they can shed some light on what he was doing, if they're willing," Kaila added. If Gerald was doing anything criminal, his friends were either involved or would know something and probably weren't going to say.

They both turned around and continued searching the people on their lists.

"It's going to take forever to interview all of these people. It's possible that we could call them to come here and just interview one right after another," George suggested.

"That might work. It would sure save time not having to commute." Kaila glanced at the clock in the corner of the room. "It's almost debriefing time. Should we call and try to set up for tomorrow?"

"Sure. The sooner the better. Look who's coming," George said.

Kaila released the phone receiver as she glanced up. "He actually left his dungeon." Kaila laughed.

The tech was carrying a stack of papers and heading their way. The look he shot Kaila said he knew what she had said and she looked down to hide her smirk.

"I have something for you," he said.

"Great! You finished already?"

"Your victim wasn't very bright."

"He didn't seem like the sharpest tack in the box," George commented. "So, what did you find?"

"He had a lot of meetings in his calendar; he even had their names listed and sometimes addresses."

"So?" Kaila said.

"I'm getting to it. I recognized some of the names." He paused for affect.

"And?" Kaila asked. "From where?" It was like pulling teeth.

"From other cases. They're known for their involvement with the drug rings."

"No way! Let me see," Kaila demanded, grabbing the papers from his hand and quickly skimming them. "He was that stupid to put names? Maybe that's why he was killed…."

"He did try and delete some a couple of days ago. But I was able to retrieve them. Same with emails."

Kaila looked over at George, speculation in her eyes. "That's around the time we talked to him about the girls? Coincidence?"

"I think he got worried we would check deeper and find something," George agreed.

"I guess we have some associates to talk to now. Let's get to the meeting and we can decide after what our next move will be," Kaila suggested.

"Sounds good," George said.

They were the last to arrive at the debriefing.

"OK, let's get started. What do you have to report about Rachel?" George asked.

The detective cleared his throat before saying, "So far, we haven't found anything different from your results. Her parents aren't very forthcoming. They still don't have any suspects; everyone loves them, supposedly. Their self-opinion is very high."

His partner snorted in agreement. "We found a few more friends and they had nothing new. Rachel had no enemies; she dated a few guys from school. No issues or problems. Her work, same thing, though her boss remembered a customer a couple of months ago that harassed Rachel. But he didn't know the guy; he was kicked out and hasn't returned."

"Did any of her coworkers remember this piece of work?" George questioned.

"Nope."

"What about her parents? Did you have a chance to ask them about this guy?"

"No, we just found this out at the end today before coming here. We'll check with them later."

"Anything else?"

The detective flipped through his pad before saying, "No."

"OK, what about Victoria?"

"It's the same with us. No one can think of anything to help. As you have in your notes, there were just the few kids in Delia's popular group at school who harassed her. We were able to identify them and tracked down most of their whereabouts, and they were on holidays at the time of her murder. The girls swear it was just a joke and that they have matured in the last couple of years."

Kaila could hear the skepticism in his voice. George looked at Kaila and nodded.

"We've talked with Gerald's parents and they don't know any suspects. They did give us a list of his friends and his laptop. We just found out that he has appointments in his computer, which he tried to delete. There are some known drug criminals." Kaila paused as she watched surprise pass over the other detectives' faces.

"So, is that why he was killed?"

"We're not sure. We'll interview them all next. But we're thinking Gerald still somehow relates to the girls' cases. Also, some of his friends are in the system for petty crimes."

"Could the girls have gotten involved in with what Gerald was up to? Or even stumbled across and were eliminated?"

"That's a possibility; we'll give you Gerald's friends list for you to check with your investigations. See if there's a connection."

As they volleyed ideas back and forth, Kaila could feel the one officer's glare focused on the back of her head, but when she swiveled around, he just had a bland expression on his face. She breathed a sigh of relief when the meeting was over and they all headed back to their desks. Kaila felt like she was developing a twitch between her shoulder blades.

"Should we keep calling his friends for interviews for tomorrow?" Kaila asked, walking back to their desks.

"Yes. Let's get that settled."

"We also need to find Gerald's associates and see if they have alibis."

Kaila pulled into the Wendy's drive-thru and ordered chili and a baked potato. She could feel her stomach grumbling as the cars crawled along the line at a snail's pace and Kaila muttered under her breath, glancing at the clock again. Eight o'clock already. She would just have time to go home and eat and collapse into bed. It would be a long day again tomorrow interviewing all the friends and associates, and she needed to be alert.

Chapter 22

Kaila arrived first at the station. *Where could George be?* Kaila thought with surprise. She started organizing their papers to ensure everything would be ready. The first interview was at eight o'clock. Some of Gerald's friends had to work, surprise!

"We ready to go?" George asked as he hurried into the station.

"Yep. Hopefully one of his friends can give us some answers."

"Who's first?"

Kaila looked down at her paper. "Looks like it's Toby."

"Is he one of the crooks?"

"Not that I know of, he doesn't have a record."

"Do we have all the interviews one right after the other?"

"Almost, the last couple we'll do separate and one of the girlfriends we'll have to interview at her home."

"How come?"

"She was busy today. I think she was working."

"I think our first contestant is here."

Kaila turned to watch a young man saunter their way, led by a detective.

"Detectives, Toby's here for his interview."

"Thanks." Kaila smiled and motioned to the chair beside her desk. The detective walked away as Toby sat beside Kaila.

"Thanks for coming, Toby," Kaila said.

"No problem. Whatever I can do."

"When was the last time you saw Gerald?" George asked.

"A couple of nights ago. We went out to the bar."

"How many were there?" Kaila asked.

Toby was silent for a minute before saying, "There were five of us."

"Did you meet at the club?"

"Yeah, Gerald said he had things to do."

"He didn't say what?"

"No, and I didn't ask."

"Can you write down their names?" Kaila asked, pushing a pad of paper towards Toby. "How was he that night?"

"He seemed fine."

"He wasn't upset or acting different?"

"Not that I noticed."

"What did you guys discuss?"

"Oh, you know, the usual, guy things."

"What about his work, any problems there that you're aware of?"

"No. He's a bouncer and bartender though. I'm sure he's ticked off some people, but enough to kill?" Toby shook his head.

"Was he involved with drugs?"

"I–I don't know." Toby said nervously.

"We know he associated with drug dealers, we just want to know the extent."

"I don't get involved with that side of his life. We're just high school buddies. Nothing serious ever happens when I'm around."

"OK, thanks for your help. If you think of anything else, please give us a call." Kaila held out her card as Toby stood up.

"Well, nothing learned there," George said.

Kaila sighed as she jotted down her notes. "At least we're not having to drive for nothing. We need to send someone to check for Gerald's car at the bar and the surrounding area."

"I'll set it up. Who's next?"

"Let me check; Carter. He's one of our little thieves."

"How much time do we have?"

"If on time, about fifteen minutes."

"OK, I'm going to grab a coffee, do you want one?"

"Sure; what's wrong with our lovely stuff over there?" Kaila laughed.

George grunted as he grabbed his coat. "If you like syrup, it's fine."

Kaila finished researching Carter and writing the questions she wanted to ask. Kaila could feel a headache coming on and rubbed her forehead with a sigh. A large coffee cup dropped in front of her and Kaila smiled in relief. *Ahh, caffeine.* She took a large sip.

"Thanks, George."

"No prob. Has the twerp shown up yet?"

"Not that I know of.... Oh, he looks like a real winner."

They watched as a young man swaggered towards them. His bandana held back long greasy bangs. He wore low-rise ripped jeans with his underwear peeking out the top, and a smirk across his face.

"How old is he supposed to be?" George muttered.

"Twenty-one."

"So, you're Kaila?" Carter asked with a leer.

195

"That's Detective Porter. Please have a seat."

Carter slouched in the chair, crossed his arms and stared at them.

"OK, so how did you know Gerald?" George asked.

"From around."

"Did you go to school with him?"

Carter snorted and looked down at himself. "I don't think so. I left after tenth grade."

"When's the last time you saw Gerald?"

"A couple of nights ago."

"You were out with him at the bar?"

"No." He laughed. "I saw him earlier."

"Do you know if Gerald was involved with drugs?"

"Oh, he did recreationally. There's no harm in that."

Kaila just looked at him for a moment. "Do you know if he had any that night?"

"Yeah, a little."

"Does he have any enemies or issues with people?"

"Oh, I could believe there are people with an axe to grind with him."

"How come?"

"He knew how to tick people off, and enjoyed it."

"Was there anyone that night?"

"Not when I was there, but I left probably around nine."

"Where did you guys meet?"

"At one of his friend's house, I think his name was Toby."

"Did Gerald tell you what his plans were for the rest of the night?"

"After he finished a smoke, he was going out with the guys to their regular haunt."

"Why didn't you go?"

"I don't really get along with some of his acquaintances. And I had other plans with a chick."

"With a chick?" Kaila asked.

"Yeah. We were hanging out, if you know what I mean."

Kaila tried to keep the disgust off her face. "Can you think of anything else about him that may help?"

"Not really. Anyway, I have to scram."

"Give us a call if you think of anything," George said, standing up with him.

"Sure. Whatever."

"It sounds like Gerald was a winner. We might have a few suspects to talk with. And I don't think I'm surprised that Toby was lying to us. How could he not know Gerald was doing drugs at his house; and what else wasn't he telling us?"

"This is going to be a long day," George commented.

By noon, Kaila was starving and ready to pull out her hair. They were learning some interesting tidbits about Gerald, and many of them weren't good. So maybe the cases weren't related.

"Let's go eat, I'm starving. And I can't stare at these notes anymore," Kaila stated.

"I'm with you. These little punks are getting on my last nerve. I'll probably strangle the next one that comes in."

"Well, it's one of his girlfriends after lunch. Not sure if she'll know anything useful."

Once they had their food, Kaila asked, "So, I'm getting confused. The girls were model citizens, no complaints, no suspects. Their only suspicious friend is Gerald. But, of course, it sounds like he could have a lot of potential enemies that aren't related to the girls' cases. They were killed in somewhat similar manner, but

Gerald's was more violent. Are they really the same cases?"

"I'm not sure either anymore," George agreed.

"Me too. I wonder if the other teams have been able to find anything more concrete to connect them."

"Well, here's to hoping," George said, raising his cup.

Chapter 23

"Daddy! Daddy!" The sound was music to his ears. He held out his arms and braced himself. Two whirlwinds slammed into his body and he pulled them close. He blinked back the tears that threatened to fall.

"Why didn't you come sooner?" the kids demanded.

"I'm sorry. I've been busy taking care of some things." He felt a shadow fall over them. *It was the bitch!* he thought to himself and fixed a hard smile on his face as he looked up.

"Where have you been?" she demanded. Her voice grated on his nerves and he wanted to strike out so bad. But he had to wait; the time must be right.

"You look terrible. Maybe you shouldn't take them."

The man slowly stood up and put the kids behind him. "I...am...fine. We're leaving," he said menacingly.

He saw her take a step back and a look of fear flickered across her face. But she then stood taller and said, "Fine, but you better be back in four hours," she threatened before stomping off.

The man turned around triumphantly and gazed at his kids. They were his life, and no one was going to take them away.

"OK, kids, let's get going." They all piled into his car and drove off as the woman watched from the safety of her living room.

Chapter 24

"Hello, Ashley. Thanks for coming," Kaila said, as she ushered the girl to the chair.

"That's fine. I feel terrible about Gerald." Ashley sniffled into her Kleenex.

She's the first that looks upset about his death, Kaila thought to herself.

"How long did you know Gerald?"

"Since ninth grade."

"So you went to the same school?"

"Yes."

"When was the last time that you saw him?"

"About a week ago. We went on a date."

"Oh, so you were dating?"

"Kind of." Ashley sighed. "We were on and off again. He didn't want to stay with just one girl. Thought he was too young."

Kaila nodded her head in agreement. "How long had it been this time?"

"Probably three months." She continued to tear at the Kleenex in her hands, not looking up.

"Ashley," Kaila waited until she looked up. "Is there something wrong?" Kaila asked gently.

"I told him to watch himself!" she began to wail. Kaila looked around wildly and grabbed a box of Kleenex, handing it over.

"What do you mean?"

"Just that he started hanging around some weird people lately." Ashley hiccupped.

"What kind of weird people?"

Ashley leaned closer and whispered, "Well, they did bad things."

"Like?"

"I'm sure they stole things and they got into drugs."

"Did you do any of that?"

"Of course not! I know better."

"OK, I'm sorry." Kaila held up her hands. "Some of the people we interviewed said that Gerald liked to tick people off; that he found it funny."

"No way! When we were together, he was the sweetest guy," Ashley denied.

"What about when you weren't on a date? When it was just the gang hanging out?"

"Well—" she hedged.

"Come on, Ashley. I need to know the truth in order to find his killer."

"He was sometimes short with people, because they were stupid. And if they didn't understand, it wasn't his fault."

"Is that him talking or you?"

"He'd say that all the time."

"Do you know anyone that would want to hurt him from work or personally?"

"I think it was one of those druggies he hung out with," Ashley said.

"Did you see them threaten him or say anything?"

"Well, no. But it's their fault he was carrying the drugs."

"You mean, he was dealing?"

"I don't know. But he seemed to always have some. And sometimes he would stop to talk to these people."

"He didn't have any on him when he was found."

"Maybe he was giving it up," Ashley said hopefully, clasping her hands. "That's why they killed him," she pronounced.

"Can you think of anyone else?"

"No."

"What about Rachel or Victoria. Were they involved with Gerald?"

"I don't think so, those bitches!"

"What do you mean?" Kaila asked with surprise.

"They were always hanging around, they wanted Gerald for themselves," Ashley pronounced loudly.

"Both of them? From what Gerald said, they were just friends," Kaila asked skeptically.

"Of course. He was a great catch." Ashley's voice caught at the end and she wiped her eyes. "Gerald was a man, he wouldn't notice a girl having a crush on him."

Kaila shook her head slightly before saying, "Thanks again, Ashley, and I'm sorry for your loss. Can you please, don't go around saying you think it was some of his more unsavory friends. I don't want you getting into any trouble."

"I guess. I don't know if I can keep it in, though."

"Please try. Here's my card in case you think of anything else."

Ashley took the card and wobbled out to the front of the station. *Oh, that could get ugly*, Kaila thought, shaking her head. She finished typing her notes and then began looking up Gerald's work. He worked at a bar called The Jazz Club for the past couple of years, in many capacities. The club had been open for ten years and catered to the rich kids. Kaila checked her watch and wondered what was taking George so long with his interview; hopefully that was a good sign, but maybe not. *The kid is probably dead at the table, and George is deciding how to hide him,* Kaila thought wryly. At that moment, George walked into her sight; or should she say stomped. And yes, he looked mad.

"Is there a body we have to clean up?" Kaila asked.

"No, but it was close."

"What was taking so long?"

"The kid rambled worse than my father ever did. About nothing, and when I was about to shoot him, he clammed up."

"What did you say to him?" Kaila asked, trying not to laugh.

"Nothing! We were discussing that night at the club and how Gerald was an ass. Of course, but not always...for sure, though, that night. That was how the kid was talking." George collapsed into his chair and dropped his head.

"Take a couple of deep breaths."

George raised his head and glared at Kaila, "How did yours go?"

"Fine. I had the crying one."

"Someone actually cared that he was gone?" George asked in shock.

"Yes. And she was blaming his drug friends. Quite loudly. I cautioned her on not doing that."

"Yeah, otherwise we might have another body."

"She also thought both Rachel and Victoria wanted Gerald for themselves."

"Really. She must be delusional." George snorted.

"So, do you want to go clubbing tonight?"

"I guess. For that I need to get some rest. After our briefing, I'm heading out. Did you discover where Gerald's other friends are? We should talk with them."

"I need to call someone in the drug division and see if they have any known location for them."

Kaila hung up the phone and turned to George with a smile, "They're emailing me the locations."

"Good, I want to get going."

Kaila drummed her fingers, waiting for the response.

Charles Hubbard was on the drug division's radar, and he was friends with Gerald, or at least an acquaintance. The email came through and she opened it. Charles choice of haunts was schoolyards and he also frequented Glenmore Park, her area.

"Are we going to find him?" Kaila asked.

"Yes, we need to eliminate him as a suspect. Do you have a picture of him?"

"I printed it off," Kaila answered, handing it over. George studied it for a moment before pushing up from his seat.

They surveyed the park from the truck, scanning for Charles. "Do you see him?" Kaila asked.

"No, do you?"

"I guess we're going for a stroll." Kaila sighed as she shivered.

"Let's split up, but keep in eyesight."

Kaila started walking, her eyes swiveling back and forth. Farther ahead, Kaila glimpsed someone who looked like Charles. She quickly texted George and waited for a response. He was going to circle around, so Kaila waited before approaching him. She was almost upon him when she said, "Charles, do you have a minute?"

A look of surprise crossed his face and he froze, but not for long, and then he was off. Kaila wasn't far behind and was closing the distance when George stepped out of the trees and tackled him. Kaila stopped beside them and bent over, breathing a little heavily; her jacket was heavy and warm. George cuffed Charles and yanked him up.

"Why did you run?" Kaila demanded. "I just had a few questions."

"Cops don't just have questions." He scowled.

"Come on, we're going for a little ride to the station," George stated as he pulled Charles back to the truck.

George took the handcuffs off of Charles and pushed him into a chair in the interview room. Charles crossed his arms and watched them.

"We want to know about Gerald Radcliff," Kaila said.

"Who?"

"Gerald. He had your name in his calendar," George responded, pushing the picture towards him.

"That dumbass!" Charles snarled.

"So, where were you two days ago?"

"Why?"

"Because Gerald is dead and he could have ticked you off."

"Hey, no way," he denied vehemently, shaking his head, holding his hands up.

"Then tell us where you were."

"Fine. I was at home."

"Alone?"

"Yes. But I ordered pizza at midnight."

"Write down your information," Kaila said, pushing the paper towards him.

Charles scribbled furiously before handing it back.

"How do you know Gerald?"

"From around."

"Specifics if you want to be cleared," George said.

Charles glared at them and said, "At his club."

"Was he working for you?"

"No. I didn't really trust him."

"Why not?"

"Because he couldn't keep his mouth shut."

"So, did he do something for you?"

"Nothing serious. He helped out now and then."

"Did he piss you off?" George asked.

"Not enough to kill him. That little shit wasn't worth it."

"Would it have been for someone else?"

"I don't know anything about that," Charles said.

"We'll check this out and get back to you. Don't move," Kaila said, grabbing the paper.

"Have we gotten the autopsy yet?" Kaila asked.

George glanced around his desk, "Not yet. Hopefully soon."

"I'll follow up on this." Kaila waved the paper.

Vern's Pizza was where Charles had supposedly ordered his pizza. Kaila looked up the number closest to his address and dialed. She was transferred to three different people before getting the information she requested. Kaila hung up the phone, "Well, Charles was telling the truth. He ordered at eleven-thirty and it was delivered at twelve-fifteen. Of course, he never gave a tip, the cheap bastard. Not my words."

"I guess release him for now. Hopefully we'll get the autopsy soon with time of death," George said.

Kaila nodded in agreement and left to give Charles the good news.

Later, Kaila said, "I don't think we have time to stop at Gerald's other friend."

George glanced at his watch. "Yeah, I want to go home first before we go out tonight. Let's talk to her tomorrow."

"Sounds fine. I'm going to finish investigating these people in Gerald's computer."

The first thing Kaila did once arriving at home was grab Echo's leash and head to the park. She hadn't been out in days with him and he was going nuts. During the run, Kaila reviewed the interviews from that day, coming up with multiple suspects. First none, and then too many to count on this case. Echo ran into another snow bank, barking like crazy, pulling Kaila along with him. She grimaced as the snow began to seep into her running shoes and dragged him back onto the somewhat clear path. It was still early enough that they had to dodge around other joggers.

From what the other detectives had reported, none of the girls' friends or relatives knew any of Gerald's acquaintances. So they were off to the club to check for any leads on the parents. Hopefully tonight turned something up at Gerald's work.

Kaila and Echo stumbled into the apartment building and rested against the wall for the elevator. She let Echo loose in the living room as she had a quick shower before searching the fridge for something to make. Kaila grabbed the egg carton, cheese and some veggies. A great aroma was wafting in the kitchen when Holly walked in.

"Oh, that smells good. Have any extra?"

"Sure, sit down. I'll whip up some more."

"I'm not going to say no." Holly laughed as she grabbed a plate and held it out towards the frying pan.

"Are you just finishing up work? Or were you at school?" Kaila asked.

"School. I have some projects due next week."

"How is it?" Kaila asked, nodding to the plate.

"Delicious," Holly replied while stuffing in another mouthful. Kaila grinned and turned back to the stove, flipping her omelet before it burned.

"What are your plans for the night?" Holly asked.

"George and I are going clubbing."

"No! I assume it's for a case?" Holly smiled.

"We're going to check out Gerald's work. I'm sure George is looking forward to it."

"Do you think you're going to run into any more interesting characters?"

"Hey, you said you wouldn't bring that up again," Kaila threatened with the spatula.

"Sorry, I just couldn't help it." Holly laughed, holding up her hands in surrender.

"It's not my fault I didn't know about people like that," Kaila grumbled as she sat down.

Holly kept her head down, trying to keep the grin off her face.

The girls were watching the news when Kaila's phone beeped.

"That's probably George," Kaila said as she checked. "Yep, he's raring to go paint the town red."

"I wonder if he did it back in his day," Holly asked.

"I don't know. He doesn't talk about his younger years. But from what I've seen, if you have a real strict adult, many times it means they were wild as a kid. I'll have to eventually wring it out of him; it would be interesting to know."

"I'd like to know some of those stories; he seems like quite a character."

"He is. I'd better finish getting ready or he'll probably leave me behind."

Kaila pulled on a pair of her skintight jeans, a sweater and her cowboy boots, and she was out the door. George was waiting outside of the apartment, drumming his fingers on the steering wheel.

"Did you text me when you were sitting out here already?"

"No, I've only been waiting a minute. I just want to get this over with."

Kaila looked George over. "Well, at least you're not dressed in your suit anymore."

"Haha. I do have clothes other than the ones I wear to the station. I was quite the fashion guy when younger, you know."

"Oh really," Kaila said, trying not to laugh.

"Hey, no laughing, or I'll make you do all the paper work."

"Fine, fine. I believe you."

George muttered under his breath as they pulled into traffic.

Chapter 25

"Where have you been!" she screeched in his face, opening the door for the children to run by.

The man grabbed the bitch's arm and twisted as he snarled, "We were having fun. You're lucky I brought them back. Don't you *ever* talk to me like that again."

"Or what?" She cried in pain and managed to yank her arm free.

"You'll regret it."

"You can't threaten me," she said, and tried closing the door in his face.

The man wedged his foot between the door and the frame and a look of terror crossed her face.

"Don't push me, bitch! Especially in front of my kids. Remember what happened before?" he snarled quietly.

"Fine! Just get out and leave me alone!" She was able to push his foot out and slammed the door.

The man stood fuming for a moment contemplating if he should finish it now. Taking a calming breath, he decided he couldn't, there were still things he needed to arrange. There was planning, but soon it would all be over. She would be sorry. Soon.

The woman stood pressed against the door, tears streamed down her cheeks as she listened to the retreating steps of the man. Her heartbeat slowed, going back to normal. She pasted a smile on her face, wiped the tears away and headed towards her children.

Chapter 26

As they pulled up in front of The Jazz Club, the sun was setting behind the buildings, casting shadows where the people stood in line. Loud music poured out every time the door opened and the people strained to get a glimpse inside. It was like they thought something was happening that they would miss. Kaila sauntered up to the bouncer and leaned in close to be heard.

"We need to get in." Before she could continue, the bouncer started shaking his head, even though he checked her out with a smile.

"Listen to the lady," George growled, pushing his way in front and flashing his badge in the man's face.

"Enjoy yourself." He opened the rope and waved them through amidst the mutterings of the waiting people behind them.

A shockwave of noise blasted them as they entered. Trying to weave their way to the bar through the gyrating kids was like swimming in quicksand and George just gave up and began to push his way through. Kaila stuck close behind or else she would be lost. He grabbed a seat at the bar and waved the bartender over.

"Hello, we're here to ask questions about Gerald. Who can we talk to?" George flashed his badge.

"I'll get the manager. Just wait here." The bartender left and walked to the back behind a curtain. Kaila turned around and watched as the people danced their hearts out. Sweat glistened on their slightly glazed faces as the lights flashed all around and skimpily dressed girls danced on the speakers. Many of the patrons looked a lot younger than eighteen, but she wasn't here for that. Nowadays, people were looking younger and younger. Many of the new recruits at the station didn't look a day over sixteen.

Kaila remembered when she was that age and there were quite a few underage kids sneaking into bars. Not that there was really anything in Cremona; they ended up traveling to Calgary when they wanted to party. It's kind of hard to sneak in when everyone in town knows who you are.

"Follow me." The bartender had returned and was motioning for them to follow.

As Kaila turned, she felt a hand on her arm.

"Hey, where are you going? Come and dance." Kaila glanced back and saw a young man grinning in her direction.

"Sorry, I can't. I'm here on business."

"Well, when you're finished, come and find me."

"I just might." Kaila smiled back at him before hurrying after George.

They were stopped at a small brown door as the bartender peeked his head inside before ushering them in. Behind the large oak desk sat a small, unassuming man. He was going bald and had large rim glasses perched on the end of his nose. Kaila glanced in surprise at George before sitting in one of the plush leather chairs. She ran her hands along the smooth surface, trying not to sigh in pleasure. She would love to have furniture like this in her apartment, but alas, the police didn't pay enough. Eventually she would have everything she wanted; Kaila was more than willing to work hard for it. The bartender shut the door behind him as the manager stared at his unwanted guests.

George cleared his throat. "We're detectives here to ask questions about Gerald...."

"Yes, we heard about him, such a tragedy," the man said in a squeaky voice.

"How did you hear about his death?" Kaila asked.

"He didn't show up earlier today for his shift, so I called his house. Gerald's mother told me about his murder."

"Can we get your name?" Kaila asked, as she pulled out her notebook.

"Sure, it's Noel Samson. Or people call me Mouse."

Kaila just shook her head in response. If she opened her mouth, she was sure laughter would spill out.

"Was Gerald working Sunday night?" George asked.

"No, it was his night off."

"So, you didn't see him at all?"

"I didn't, but I'm not usually out there." Mouse looked down at himself. "I'm not the most appealing man. Not always good for the peak business. But my partner is out and about schmoozing the customers."

"Is he here right now?"

"No, he doesn't usually come in until eleven. He then closes up the place."

"Can we get his number?"

Mouse rattled off the phone number.

"Was there anyone harassing Gerald that you knew of?"

"No, he seemed to be able to handle himself."

"What do you mean?"

"Well, he also helped out bouncing when we needed someone."

215

"Did you see him hanging around some unusual characters?"

"What do you mean? How would they look?"

"Did they seem shifty, nervous? Were they exchanging packages?"

"Do you mean, was he dealing drugs? Not in my place. I run a clean establishment." Kaila watched as Mouse's forehead began to turn red and his nostrils flared.

"We're not saying you allowed it. We just need to figure out what happened, and that usually happens in clubs at one time or another."

Mouse muttered under his breath, "Fine, fine."

"What about girls?"

"Oh, they loved Gerald, and I'm sure he loved them as well."

"Did you notice any that were around more often than the others?"

"No, but like I said, I'm more the behind-the-scenes guy. You'll have to talk with Mitch."

"Did you have any problems with Gerald?"

Mouse paused for a moment and frowned.

"Well?" Kaila asked.

"Not really. He was sometimes belligerent, but I get that from a lot of staff. We're talking about young adults working here, and they don't have the greatest work ethic."

"You can say that again," Kaila agreed.

"What happened?" George asked.

"I caught him a couple of times leaving the bar unattended to go and make out with a girl."

"Why wasn't he fired?"

"Mitch likes him, and it's hard to get a good bartender and bouncer that the customers like." Mouse shrugged his shoulders and swigged his coffee mug. Kaila wondered if there was something stronger in there. If she worked here, something stronger would be nice.

"Have you had any complaints about him?" George asked.

"Oh, no. Like I said, the customers loved him."

"Even the guys?" Kaila said in surprise.

"Enough not to complain about him."

"Do you have any video cameras in the club?" Kaila questioned.

"Sure, we have them at all the exits and at the bar. A couple also point into the club."

"We need to see them."

"For what time period?"

"Maybe for Sunday night and if you have Gerald's last couple of shifts."

"I can get them for you. Probably won't be until tomorrow."

"That's fine. Here's my card, if you can call and let me know when they're ready. Can we talk with the other employees here?" Kaila asked.

"I guess, please just don't interrupt them if they're busy with customers."

"No problem. Thanks for your time," George said, standing up and holding out his hand.

Mouse stood up. *Though it didn't really look like it,* Kaila thought. He shook their hands before walking them to the door.

"I hope you find who did this."

"Oh, we will," Kaila responded.

They headed back through the curtain into the crowded dance floor.

"Do you want to try and talk with the bartender?" Kaila asked.

"With it this busy, it might be better if a girl did. I think you would get more cooperation. I'll head to the kitchen and find out the scoop."

"Sure, I'll meet you back out here later."

As Kaila walked towards the bar, she bumped into the guy who had asked her to dance earlier.

"Hey, gorgeous. Looking for me?"

Kaila laughed at the obvious pick-up line. "Not right now. I have to talk with the bartender."

"What, Rudy? What does he have that I don't?" Kaila watched as the twinkle in his eyes traveled down to his beautiful smile.

"Sorry, but I'm still here on business."

"That's too bad. Well, see you around." Kaila watched as he sauntered away, and gave a sigh. The work was never done.

Kaila pulled up a stool and watched as the bartender swung the bottles of liquor, pouring colorful drinks. There was a lineup of servers waiting their turn, tapping their feet to the music. Of course, all of them were young; they looked underage and curvy. Their clothes just barely covered the skin and Kaila was sure if they moved too fast, something would rip. The music seemed to be louder than when they first arrived, and if it was possible, more people were on the dance floor. Of course they couldn't really move, so it was more of a sway and the bodies bumped back and forth. She could see the sweat glistening off of some of the dancers as heat seemed to rise above them. In this day and age, you would think the clubs would have air conditioning...or maybe they just didn't use them so people would drink more. Of course, the hotter the people got, the more clothes came off, so probably good for business.

"Hey, what can I get you?"

Kaila glanced over in surprise. The bartender stood in front of her with a smile.

"Can I get a club soda please?"

"Sure. That's on the house," he said, as she pulled out her money.

"Thanks." Kaila smiled widely in his direction. "My name's Kaila," she cleared her throat and showed him her badge. "Detective Porter."

"Rudy."

"Can I ask you some quick questions?"

"If you're fast. I have lots to do."

"No prob. Can you tell me about Gerald?"

"Where do you want me to start?"

"How was he to work with?"

"A pain in the ass. He didn't do a whole lot and he was a jerk to the staff. Not sure why they didn't fire him."

"What about Sunday night; did you see him here?"

"Sure, he was here with some friends."

"How did he seem? Was he worried or scared?"

"I don't know what would scare him. He hung out with some pretty scary dudes and he seemed fine."

"Were they with him that night?"

"No, they looked like college boys. I recognized some of them as regulars."

"Did you see him leave with anyone?"

"Nope. Just his posse. Good riddance."

Kaila looked at him in shock.

"Sorry, I don't mean that he is dead, but that he left that night," Rudy said hastily.

"How come?"

"He was his loud, obnoxious self and we were busy. He expects to get everything free for him and his friends. He almost caused a fight. Sorry, I have to get back. Hope to see you around."

"Thanks." Kaila grabbed her drink and walked to one of the servers at the bar.

"Hi, I'm Detective Porter. Can I ask you a few questions about Gerald?"

"Really, you're a cop?" she said in disbelief.

"Yes, do you have a moment?"

"I guess. I didn't really care for the guy, but he didn't deserve to die." Kaila leaned in closer to hear.

"You didn't get along with him either?"

"I did at first, but he tried to pick up all the female employees and when we got wise, he became a jerk."

"So, he thought of himself as a ladies' man?"

"Oh, totally. Of course, all the female customers loved him; I think that's why they kept him around. Here's my drinks. Back to work." Kaila watched her sashay up to her table, carrying her tray high to avoid all the dancers. All the other servers were with their tables, so Kaila headed towards the kitchen to find George.

"How's it going?" Kaila asked as George walked out.

"What?"

Kaila pulled him towards an empty table in the corner.

"What did you find out?"

"That he was a jerk."

"Same here. He tried to pick up all the staff. But the customers loved him. Also, he had some real winners as friends."

George waved away the server before saying, "It sounds like a love-hate relationship. I wonder if we should wait around until Mitch shows up? Or should we just try calling him tomorrow?"

Kaila glanced at her watch; it was eleven. "Why don't you head out? I might stick around for a bit and I can talk to him. If he doesn't show, we can call tomorrow. I also wasn't able to talk with all the servers."

"You're sure?" George asked in relief.

"Yeah, get out of here," Kaila said, trying not to laugh.

"OK, I'll see you in the morning. Stay out of trouble," he warned.

"Always." Kaila watched George exit the club before heading back to the bar. It was time to have a little fun.

Chapter 27

"You made it in," George joked as Kaila flopped in her chair.

"Of course. I'm still young, I can handle it." Kaila took a long swig of her coffee and grimaced.

"How did it go last night?"

"Fine. Mitch showed up about midnight, and then to get his undivided attention was painful."

"What did he have to say?"

"Nada."

"What!"

"Gerald is a great guy. Doesn't believe he dealt drugs, 'must be a mistake.' Blah, blah, blah."

"His exact words?" George grinned.

"Yep, word for word. Except the beginning, I paraphrased."

"What's he like?"

"The exact opposite of Noel. I guess that's why he's the face of the club. He has schmoozing down to a science, especially with the ladies."

George snorted. "That's what I figured. Did he see Gerald the night of his murder?"

"Yes, but 'Gerald was being an angel and left quietly with his friends.'"

"I'm going to call Noel soon about the tape. We'll know the truth then."

"You know, from everything we've found, it seems like there are plenty of motives for Gerald's death. No one in the girls' lives is suspicious."

"We will wait to hear back from the other detectives about the club and any issues with the parents."

"We have to be missing something. To have two best friends killed at random is not common."

"I'm going to give Noel a call," George said, as he grabbed the phone. "I'm not waiting any longer."

Kaila sipped her coffee as she listened to the one-sided conversation. There were a few explosive words before George slammed the phone down.

"Well?" Kaila asked.

"We can go pick it up. He's found it."

"Did he say if there's anything on them?" Kaila asked as she grabbed her jacket.

"He supposedly didn't watch it."

"Yeah, right. Well, let's get there before the film is changed."

When they arrived at the club, Noel was waiting for them in the front.

"Here's the USB. I'll need it back," Noel demanded.

"Once the investigation is complete; it's evidence right now," Kaila answered as she took the USB.

"Thanks. We'll be in touch," George said as they walked out.

"So, what are you expecting to find?" Kaila asked.

"Not sure. It would be nice, but I don't think we're going to find our killer."

"How come?" Kaila looked at him in surprise.

"Because the way our luck is going."

Kaila sighed as she nodded her head in agreement.

"Should we see if the others are here?" Kaila asked as they walked into the station.

"Good idea, I'll set up in the meeting room."

Kaila went to round up the rest of the team. Not everyone was in, but they got three of them, including the chief.

"We received the surveillance video from the night of Gerald's murder. Hopefully there's something."

George started the video and sat back. The time and date told them the club had already been open for a couple of hours. It was nine o'clock.

"Do we know what time Gerald arrived?" one of the detectives asked.

Kaila flipped through her notes, "Nope, Toby hadn't said."

They watched as customers came and went; nothing exciting happened. At ten, Kaila sat up and pointed, "There they are."

"There's Toby," George commented.

Gerald and his friends sat at a table close to the bar and the detectives watched as Gerald started yelling for service.

"What an ass," one of the detectives said.

"I know. You would think he'd be nicer to his coworkers," Kaila agreed.

"Hey, Carter's not supposed to be there," Kaila said, writing on her pad. She glanced back at the time— eleven-fifteen p.m. Gerald and Carter got up and walked towards the bathroom and out of sight of the camera. Ten minutes later, Gerald came back alone and sat at the table. He continued to be obnoxious until midnight when he almost got into a fight with another customer and was asked to leave.

225

"Why do they let him continue working there?" Kaila asked in wonder, watching Gerald and his friends stumble towards the front door. "I know Noel said he was liked by the customers, but really."

They watched the video for about ten more minutes. The man who had the altercation with Gerald never left.

"Do we have any video from outside?" the chief asked.

"No, but we haven't canvassed the other businesses on that street," George answered.

"We also got video from his last couple of shifts which we can scan and see if there's anyone suspicious," Kaila said, glancing at the paper where Noel had written down Gerald's hours. She passed it on to George who rewound to that timeframe.

They had a fun-filled couple of hours searching the tapes for any suspects, but nothing came of it.

"That was a waste of time," George commented.

"I can see why the owners want to keep him around. The customers do like him, there didn't seem to be any customers having an issue with him. They're joking and laughing with him," Kaila said.

"Is anyone going back to the country club today?" George asked.

"We are. We'll check about the parents and see if there's anything going on with them."

"Sounds good. We'll talk with the rest of Gerald's friends and try getting more videos of the street."

They all stood up and headed their separate ways.

"I wonder why Carter lied," Kaila asked as she sat at her desk.

"I can just guess what they were doing. I don't think he wanted to admit to that," George answered.

"Yeah, I guess. So, we'll split up the businesses on the street and see if they have any videos. Do you want me to track down Carter, or do you want the pleasure?"

"If you want to write up the lists, I'll search for his friends. And I guess I can talk with Carter," George said with a great sigh.

Kaila laughed as she pulled up the street on Google Maps and zoomed in, writing down the surrounding companies. There were only four companies close enough that could have videos that would be worthwhile.

"Here are your two." Kaila handed over the paper she ripped off her pad.

George looked at the names. "Are you calling more?"

"No, there just aren't many."

"Great," George muttered. "There's not going to be many options here."

Kaila grimaced in agreement and continued checking out the location and searching her businesses.

George was nowhere to be seen when she dumped his burger on his desk. Kaila wasn't going to wait. She lovingly pulled out the chili and potato from her bag and sat down to eat. The first bite was heaven and her stomach seemed to agree, bringing a smile to her face. Kaila was halfway finished before George made an appearance, carrying a cup of coffee.

"Where've you been?" Kaila asked.

"Just talking with the captain."

"Everything alright?"

"Yes. Thanks for the burger."

"No problem."

Kaila finished up with her lunch and then began calling, looking for videos. It really surprised her that in this day and age that every business didn't have cameras out. They were so small that criminals wouldn't notice them. After striking out, Kaila decided to try and get ahold of Gerald's other drinking buddies. She had their names from Toby.

"Anything your way?" George asked, startling Kaila and she jumped. George chuckled as she glared his way. "Did you find any video?" George asked again, with a grin.

"No. None of them had surveillance out on the street. I hit a dead end. What about you?"

"One restaurant across the street said we could look at their video. Not sure if it will help."

"That's great news! Are you going to pick it up?"

"Yes. What are you doing?"

"I thought it would be exciting to track down Gerald's friends from that night and question them."

"I think I prefer my task. Have fun." George snickered as he walked away.

Kaila watched George head out of the station. *Good, maybe we're finally going to catch a break in the case.*

Chapter 28

The man stared down at the three plane tickets in his hands. It was just about time. Only one more thing to accomplish and he could leave this hellhole for good. He could raise his kids far away from his problems; there would be no one to stop him.

Tomorrow night would be the last for the bitch. The kids may miss her for a while, but it wouldn't last. He knew she had her weekly parent meeting at the school that ended at eight o'clock. That would be a good time to meet her for a little talk.

He giggled at that—a little talk; she wouldn't be saying much anymore. Maybe he would sew her mouth shut—or glue. He wasn't much of a seamstress. He wrote super glue down on his list along with rope and tape. He had enough garbage bags. He looked around his cabin fondly; he would miss this place when he left. It wasn't much to look at, but it was his haven, the place he had made his own.

He grinned as he pictured the bitch's face and knew this time would be the most satisfying. He didn't know if he could wait another day, but he needed patience. The best chance he had was tomorrow, and he could feel the others agreeing.

Chapter 29

While George was absent, Kaila researched the rest of Gerald's friends, but didn't find anything significant. None of them had a record. Kaila began calling them to arrange a meeting. She was just hanging up with the last call when George walked back in.

"Hey, I got it." George waved the USB with a grin. He shook the snow off his jacket before hanging it up and pushing the USB into his computer. Kaila rolled her chair over and stared at the screen.

"How exciting, more videos," Kaila said, trying to smile. "So, they just gave this over? No warrant?"

"Nope. They wanted to help out, said they had nothing to hide."

George had to scroll through the previous days before they got to the right one.

"What time did they leave the club?" George asked.

"It was midnight."

"Here's 11:00. There's the group that had the fight with Gerald."

"I don't see anyone hanging around. Hey, that car has been sitting there an awful long time."

"Which one?" George peered closer to the grainy picture.

"The one at the left corner. You can just make out the back end of it." Kaila pointed.

"Maybe the person is in one of the other buildings."

"At this time of night? Most of them are closed. Rewind the tape for me. I don't remember seeing anyone leaving the vehicle."

"You can't see the driver door, they could have been walking away from the camera."

"I know; just humor me."

"Sure." George slowly rewound the video as they kept watch of the car.

"See, it parked at ten-thirty; I didn't notice anyone walking from there. Rewind a bit more." Kaila said excitedly.

"That looks like the same vehicle driving by as Gerald is going into the club."

"You're right, George. Do you think they were following him?" Kaila gripped her chair arms as shivers shot down her spine.

"It almost looks like it. Did we look at the businesses on that side of the club?"

"Let me check the map, I'm not sure how far away I looked." Kaila scooted back to her desk and pulled up the Google map on her computer.

"There is a bookstore in front of where the car is parked and there's a meat shop and some warehouses. They're all shut down by nine. So, if the mysterious driver walked away from the club, where were they going?" Kaila asked.

"I'm not sure. Let's finish looking at the video." George fast-forwarded it to where Gerald and his friends stumbled out of the building.

"OK, there he is. Looks like his pals are heading in the opposite direction. Gerald should not be driving." Kaila frowned. "Why didn't one of his friends stop him?"

George shrugged his shoulders with a grimace.

It was hard to follow Gerald's stumbling form through the street, because the closest lamppost was across the street and it cast a very faint glow that barely reached the other side. There were plenty of shadows from the alley, and as he reached the alley, a shadow peeled away from the wall and stepped behind him. Even if Gerald had been sober, the mystery man would still have had the advantage. Kaila gasped and leaned in closer. "What the hell!"

They watched as the shadow took shape into a man, but his features couldn't be distinguished. The man hit Gerald with what looked like the butt of a gun and opened the trunk of the car. He then reached in and grabbed a rope binding up Gerald before heaving him into the trunk.

"We need to see if we can get this video cleaned up any more. I didn't see any plates on that car either," George said.

"Have we looked over Gerald's car yet? How did the kidnapper know he was there? Is there something on his car?"

"Good question. I'm not sure if we have his car in the lot yet. Why don't you find out and I'll look into the video."

George pulled out the USB stick and headed to the basement. Kaila spun to her desk and picked up her phone to dial the garage.

"Hey, can you tell me if you guys have Gerald Radcliff's car there and if you've gone through it yet," Kaila asked.

"I'm not sure, everyone else is gone. Give me a minute," the voice said and put her on hold.

Kaila drummed her fingers on the desk, waiting impatiently. She hoped that it was at least there.

"Hello?"

"Did you find it?"

"We have it here, but they haven't processed it yet."

"Can you put a rush on it for tomorrow? I need to know if there were any tracking devices on it."

"I'll make a note, but you should still call in the morning."

"OK, thanks." Kaila hung up with a sigh. The good thing was they had the car; the difficult part would be getting them to do their vehicle next.

"They'll try and clear up the video for us, but they said don't hold out a lot of hope," George said, walking back up from the dungeon. "It's not a high quality product."

"When will they get it to us?" Kaila asked.

"Should be tomorrow morning. What about you?"

"They were gone already. But the car was there. He said to call back in the morning. I'll also call the drug unit and see if they've been watching Gerald."

"Good idea, finally our luck has turned. Go home and get some sleep."

"Have you heard from the other teams?"

"Yeah, they called. I told them we'll meet in the morning. Hopefully there'll be some news to share."

Kaila groaned. "I don't want to give up yet, I feel we're so close."

"I know." George put a hand on Kaila's shoulder for a minute and she dropped her head with a sigh.

"You can't let the cases get to you, or you'll break. You have many years left."

"I understand. I'm going to meet a couple of his friends from the club before calling it a night."

Kaila trudged out to her car, almost running into a detective arriving.

"Sorry."

"No problem," he said, smiling.

She grimaced as her snow-covered car came into view and yanked out her scraper. As she swept the snow away, Kaila could picture her couch beckoning her to it. *Just a couple of more hours,* she told herself.

"Holly, are you here?"

"I'm here."

Kaila walked into the living room and found Holly sitting on the couch staring into space.

"Hey, girly, you look exhausted."

"I am," Kaila agreed and fell into the chair. "So, how come you're on my couch?" Kaila laughed.

"It's just so comfy." Holly grinned, wiggling her butt. "How's the case going?"

"I think we've hit a breakthrough."

"That's great!"

"We found Gerald's kidnapper in a video; we just need to see if we can clear it up."

"Is he connected to the girls?"

"We're not sure yet. Once we can confirm his identity, maybe then we'll know the motive."

"So nothing new on the girl's cases?"

"Not that I know of. But we have a briefing tomorrow morning. We're now looking at the parent angle."

"You think someone could be that mad with their parents to kill them?"

"It's pretty extreme, but we've hit dead ends everywhere else." Kaila got up and headed towards the kitchen. "Do you want a drink?"

"No, I'm good. Thanks."

Kaila almost tripped over Echo as he ran into the kitchen carrying his bone. Kaila smiled, picking him up for a hug.

"How you doing, boy?" Kaila asked, scratching behind his ears. Echo tried to bark around his bone and his little body quivered in excitement.

"I need to relax, you go play." Kaila set Echo down and watched as he dropped to his belly and began chewing.

"So, are you glad you moved here?" Kaila asked.

"I'm loving it, and Brian lives here."

Kaila smiled. "Have you seen him much lately?"

"We've both been real busy with work, but every couple of days."

"I'm glad," Kaila said, taking a swig of her beer with relish.

"You know, with all the work we've done in here, we should have a party."

"That sounds like a great idea! When were you thinking?"

"Maybe next Friday or Saturday?"

"Great. Do you want to have a barbeque?"

"Absolutely. How about we finish the details later," Kaila suggested, "I'm going to hit the sack."

"Alright. Good luck tomorrow."

"Thanks."

Kaila picked up Echo and headed to her room. She changed quickly, washed up and dropped into her bed. Kaila called Echo over and watched him wiggle his body over the edge of the bed, making her smile. Once he reached her, Kaila pulled his warm body under her arm and promptly fell asleep.

Kaila had tossed and turned all night. Images of the two girls kept popping up in her dreams, startling her awake. She hauled her tired body out of bed and walked to the bathroom. Staring blearily in the mirror for a minute, Kaila grabbed her hairbrush. It was easy to see the exhaustion in her face from the sleepless night.

She wanted to get to the station quickly and a shower would take too long. Kaila grabbed an apple and headed out the door. Maybe a stop at McDonalds for a coffee was in order.

"Hey, George, did you leave last night?" Kaila laughed, setting her cup down, staring into George's red eyes.

"I just got here. I wanted to get ready for the briefing."

"And you couldn't sleep," Kaila added quietly.

"And that." George grimaced.

"What do you have?"

"Why don't you get on the garage, maybe we can get some answers quickly. Did you hear back from the drug unit?"

"Not yet, I'll try them as well."

Kaila picked up the phone.

"Hello."

"Hi, this is Detective Porter. Can I get you to look at Gerald Radcliff's car? I need to know if there's a tracking device. We found a surveillance video showing Gerald being kidnapped, so we know he wasn't killed in his car, but it's crucial to know if he was followed."

"We might be able to look at it this afternoon."

Kaila grimaced. "Is there any way that you can look right away? I think it's part of a serial murder case and we're not sure if there will be another."

"We can rush it. I'll call you when we have something."

"Thanks!" Kaila hung up with a smile. "Hopefully we'll have something soon. What about you? Did you hear from IT?"

"Not yet. I might go down there and check up on them. How did your visits go last night?

"With Gerald's friends? They corroborated Toby's story. Nothing unusual happened, they were just out to

237

have a good time. I asked them about Gerald's drug use and they knew what was happening. Even though they're friends, it was agreed he could be an ass."

"So, we didn't really learn anything new."

"Nope."

"We have about an hour before the meeting," George said before walking away.

Kaila called down again to the drug unit. "Hello. This is Detective Porter. Can you tell me if Gerald Radcliff was on your radar? He's a murder victim with possible connections to two others."

"Just a minute," the detective said, putting her on hold.

About ten minutes later the voice came back on the line. "We have mention of Gerald but were not investigating him."

"So, you weren't tracking him?" Kaila asked.

"Nope."

"Do you have any information on him?"

"Only thing is, he does some minor drugs now and then, and he wasn't associated with anyone."

"OK, thanks." Kaila hung up and went through her notes on the girl's case looking for a sign of a stalker. She couldn't recall one being mentioned. It seemed like minutes before George was tapping her on the shoulder.

"Hey, time to go."

"Really? That went quick."

Once everyone was assembled, George cleared his throat. "What did you guys find out?"

"We headed back to the club yesterday and started questioning about the parents. Of course, all the staff only had good things to say about them."

"Of course, can't speak badly about the customers. But I'm surprised that there isn't at least one worker that's disillusioned and willing to gossip," Kaila said.

"Oh, we did find one of those." The detective grinned.

"Well?" Kaila asked.

"From what they heard, all three parents were working together on some investment."

"Did you find out what the investment was?" George asked, leaning forward.

"Not yet, the employee didn't know. We're going back today to question the members."

"That sounds like a promising lead, maybe one of the investors got mad," George said.

"Enough to kill their kids?" Kaila asked.

"It involves money, people will do anything for money. Maybe we'll let you finish questioning at the club before talking with the parents about the investment. We don't want to tip them off so they can threaten people to keep their mouths shut."

"What about Victoria?"

"Nothing new."

"Have any of you looked into the parents' financials?" George asked. "With their investments, there might be some transactions to follow."

"Yeah, we'll look into it." The detectives made some notes.

"We cut a break with Gerald. A surveillance video from across the street showed his kidnapping outside of the bar. I had the video cleared; it's still pretty grainy, but we have a picture." George handed out pictures of an older balding man, about six feet, with a moustache and ball cap. From what Kaila could see, he was in great shape.

"We can use this picture at the club and see if anyone recognizes him."

"The video didn't show any plates or distinguishing marks on the car?" Kaila questioned.

"The perp took the plates off," George said.

"He was taking a chance he wouldn't get pulled over by a police officer," Kaila commented.

"I guess he thought it was worth it."

"Do we have any idea of what kind of vehicle?" one of the detectives asked.

"To me it looks like it could be a Mustang," George said.

"I guess we can ask the victims' family and see if they saw this vehicle hanging around. Also, maybe taking the picture to the girls' work; see if the man came in. It's a long shot, but you never know," Kaila suggested.

"I also just got the autopsy report on Gerald." George pulled out the envelope. "They place his time of death between midnight and two a.m. He was stabbed multiple times and died of blood loss."

"Then Charles may not have had time to kill him after his pizza," Kaila said with a sigh.

Just then, there was a knock on the door and a detective stuck his head through the doorway and waved Kaila over. They whispered for a moment, and then Kaila came back with a grin.

Kaila's fan spoke up, looking directly at her. "So was Gerald being followed? Maybe you need to look into that," he said, with a superior expression on his face.

"I've already done that. I was waiting for a report from the garage about a tracking device on Gerald's vehicle and I contacting the drug unit because of his association with some known druggies. The detectives said they were aware of Gerald, but weren't tracking him. Which tells us that the tracking device our guys pulled off his car isn't one of ours," Kaila said triumphantly, holding up the report.

The detective frowned slightly while the others in the room smiled at the news.

"Good, maybe we can track it down," George said.

The group went through the rest of their findings and then split up.

Chapter 30

Today was the day. Excitement filled the man's body as he began preparing. He needed to look his best; it was going to be a special one. Everything needed to be perfect for the bitch, as it was going to be her last day alive.

First thing he did was prepare the space. He had bought a new table; more time was needed for this ending and it would be easier lying down. It was still necessary to have all the bags, so the man knelt on the floor and almost lovingly placed the bags all around and under the table. Next, he cooked a hearty breakfast; he needed to keep up his strength. The man scrambled eggs, hash browns and made some toast. He then carried his plate to the new table and dug in with gusto.

Chapter 31

When Kaila reached her desk, she read the garage report.

"OK, so as we know, they didn't find any blood in Gerald's car."

George looked at Kaila expectantly.

"But surprise, surprise, they found a couple of marijuana joints under his seat."

"We're going to have to tell his parents about the drugs," George said quietly.

"I know; it's going to break their hearts."

"Did they find anything else?"

"Just the tracking device. I wonder how long it was there. Was he being stalked for a while? How long did the killer have this planned for?"

"Well, let's call his parents, we need some answers."

"I'll give them a call. I also want to look into the tracking device that our perp used."

Kaila first tried contacting the Radcliffs, but with no luck. She left a message. Just as she hung up the phone, it rang. "Hello."

"Hi, this is Mr. Walker. I wanted to know if you found the killer of my daughter?" he demanded.

"No, Mr. Walker. But we're following all the leads. We'll contact you the moment we have something."

"You better," he said and slammed the phone down.

Kaila set her phone down slowly and looked over at George. "That was Mr. Walker."

"What did he want?"

"To find out about the case."

"I'm surprised he called. I know they're her parents, but they just seem very cold."

"Yeah, I get that feeling, too. The Radcliffs aren't home. I left a message and will try calling back later. Maybe I can find something on this tracker while we wait."

"When we finally get ahold of the Radcliffs, we can stop at Gerald's work to show around the picture."

The tracking device used was a TK-102 mini GPS tracker. Kaila Googled the tracker and found it was supposedly easy to use and required a SIM card. It could be bought anywhere; which kind of sucked. But at least there was a partial print. There would be no way to track who owned it. *Damn*, Kaila thought. They needed to talk with Gerald's parents. She picked up the phone and dialed. After talking a few minutes, she hung up and turned to George.

"The Radcliffs are home. Let's head over before they disappear," Kaila suggested.

"Knowing these families, it's entirely possible," George agreed, grabbing the picture and standing up.

"Do you think they knew about his drugs?" Kaila asked as they walked to the front steps.

"I'm not sure. A lot of parents turn a blind eye, because they don't want to believe it's their kid. The kid could also just be good at hiding from their parents. I guess some also just don't care."

Kaila rapped on the door and looked around while she was waiting. The blinds were closed up tight and they were standing in a foot of snow from the last couple of days.

"Hello." Mr. Radcliff opened the door.

"Hi. Can we come in? We have a few questions," Kaila asked.

He opened the door wider and ushered them in. They followed him and quickly pulled off their boots before continuing on.

"What do you want to know?" he asked, sitting beside his wife.

"We're wondering if you recognized this man," George asked, taking out the picture.

"Is this who killed my boy?" Mr. Radcliff asked, pulling the picture close to his face to study. Mrs. Radcliff leaned closer, putting her glasses on.

"This is pretty grainy," she said, squinting.

"Sorry, this is the best we could clear it up," George said.

Kaila kept watching Mr. Radcliff's face for his reaction. She was sure surprise crossed it, but he shook his head no. "Sorry, I don't think so," he said, handing the picture back.

"Well...." Mrs. Radcliff said, but Kaila glimpsed Mr. Radcliff squeezing her hand. "Sorry, no, I don't know who it is," she said.

"Are you sure?" Kaila questioned.

They both shook their heads no.

"Was there anything else?" he asked.

"We found your son's car by the bar. Marijuana was found under his seat," Kaila said.

"That isn't his. It must be one of his friends!" Mrs. Radcliff shook her head vehemently.

"I'm sorry, but even his friends have said that he uses, and his prints were found on them."

Before Mrs. Radcliff could respond again, Mr. Radcliff patted her hand and shook his head. "Dear, don't. Does this have any relevance, or are you telling us this to hurt us?"

"We don't want to cause you more pain, but this may be why he was killed. We're following some leads."

"So, are you saying that the man is a drug dealer?" Mr. Radcliff pointed towards the picture.

"We're not sure yet," George answered. "We aren't eliminating any possibilities."

"Do you know what happened to him?" Mrs. Radcliff asked.

"He and some friends went to the bar he worked at. Someone must have snatched him after he left at the end of the night. We'll keep you informed with what we find, and if you have any more ideas about the man, please give us a call," Kaila said, standing up.

"What about his car? When do we get it back?" he asked.

"When we're done processing it for evidence, we'll bring it back," George said, following Kaila out.

After the door closed behind them, Kaila regarded George and said, "They're lying."

"I know. They recognized him, or at least had an idea. We need to start examining their acquaintances and maybe the others will turn something up at the club. Let's head to Gerald's work with the picture. Might just be Noel there right now, but it doesn't hurt."

"Sounds good." Kaila climbed into the truck and watched the house as George wiped the windows. A curtain moved and Kaila glimpsed Mr. Radcliff observing them before the curtain snapped shut.

What the heck is going on? Kaila thought.

George hopped in, shook himself, and snowflakes settled around the seat.

"Let's get going."

"They're watching us."

"I know."

When they arrived at the bar, a couple of the staff were already there getting ready for the evening.

"Hi, is Noel here?" Kaila asked.

"Just a minute," the girl said.

George strode up to the bartender, showing him the picture. By the time Noel strode out, George had questioned all of the staff in the room.

"Hello, detectives, what can I do for you?"

"We're wondering if you recognized this man," George asked, holding out the picture.

Noel scrutinized the picture for a minute before handing it back. "Sorry, I don't. Like I said, though, I don't see many of the customers."

"It was a long shot, but we wanted to try."

As they were marching out, George's phone rang. "Hello."

Kaila watched as surprise crossed George's face and his mouth widened into a grin.

"Well?" Kaila demanded when he hung up.

"Some of the other members at the club said the guy could be Frank Larson. He's a member, or was. The family hasn't been around for some time, no one knows why. I have his home address. Do you want to get a glimpse? Hopefully it's our guy."

"Hell yes!"

They rushed out to the truck and George sped away. Thirty minutes later, they pulled up to an unassuming green house that had seen better days. Kaila could tell someone had tried to keep the yard clean and tidy. She stepped over the snowdrifts in front of the gate, strolled up to the door and rang the bell.

A woman answered the door. "Hello."

"Hi, we're wondering if Frank is in," George asked, flashing his badge.

A look of surprise crossed her face. "Sorry, he doesn't live here anymore."

"This is the address on his driver's license," Kaila said.

"We split up a bit ago. He left and I'm not sure where he's living now. Sorry." She then closed the door.

Kaila gazed over at George, "Well, I guess we were told. Let's head back to the station and I can pull up some information on Frank."

Kaila typed Frank Larson into her computer and waited.

"Oh, looky at this."

"What?" George asked, spinning around in his chair.

"There were a couple of reports of domestic violence, but no charges. His wife wouldn't press charges at the end. But I guess at least she kicked out his ass."

"Yeah, that's one thing. What else is there?"

"Nothing. He owns his own construction company, Larson Contracting." Kaila answered. "Should I call first to see if he's there or do we want to surprise him?"

"I think we should show up. We don't want to tip him off if he's our guy."

"It seems like everyone on this case is a potential runner, from our good guys to the bad," Kaila complained. "Do you think it's him?" Kaila asked as they drove away.

"The picture is poor quality, but it's our best lead so far. I'm kinda hoping. So where are we going?"

"His office is in the southeast on 114 Avenue."

"Great. That'll take a while," George grumbled.

They pulled up to Frank's office and stared at the darkened building.

"Crap! It's only quarter to four." George swore. Kaila sighed and rubbed her neck.

"What now?" Kaila asked.

"Let's go back to his wife's house."

"Sure, why not. I haven't had enough of traffic today. Let me go and knock just to make sure no one's there." Kaila opened the door to howling winds. She peered through the glass door as she pounded, hoping that someone was there, or her freezing would be pointless. Just as Kaila was about to give up, an older woman came into view. She had her white hair pulled into a bun and was wearing the same old-fashioned flower dress Kaila's grandma used to wear, no matter the weather.

"Sorry, we're closed," she said cautiously through the door.

Kaila held up her badge. "Can my partner and I come in for a few minutes, we have some questions," Kaila yelled.

The woman paused a moment before she stepped forward and turned the latch. Kaila glanced back at George and waved him in.

"What can I do for you?"

"Thanks, ma'am, can I get your name for the record?" Kaila asked, holding the door open for George.

"It's Marian Shell."

"Have you worked here long?"

"For ten years now. Why?"

Kaila nodded at George and he pulled out the picture. "Do you know this man?"

Marian took the picture and studied it for a few minutes. "That looks like Mr. Larson. Where was this taken?"

"Do you know where he is right now?"

"No, sorry, he phoned in a couple of days ago and said he would be gone till next week."

"Do you know where he lives? He broke up with his wife, right?"

"Yes, it devastated him. For a while he was sleeping in the back, but now I'm not sure."

"Can you give us his number, we would really like to talk with him."

"Alright. Is he in trouble?" she asked, writing the number down.

"We just need to talk with him. Have you noticed anything different with Mr. Larson? Has he been more agitated or upset?"

"He's been like that for a while since the divorce. But he tries to keep it out of the workplace. He's a great boss," Marian said.

"Well, thank you for your help, you have a good evening," Kaila said and headed out.

"Let's boot it back to his ex's house. Perhaps she's home and knows where he is."

"It might be better to wait till later, it's rush hour right now and they have kids. She could be out picking them up from activities or school."

"How about seven o'clock, then."

"That's better. I can do some research back at the station."

"Or you can take a quick break. I think it's going to be a late night. It's at times like these that I wish Calgary wasn't so big," George said.

"How come?"

"Because it takes so long. What else did you find out about him?"

"They were married for fifteen years and they have a boy and girl, twelve and nine years old. They've been members of the club for a little over a year, but haven't been around much. I'm guessing perhaps it's because they broke up."

"It costs a lot to be members there. How could he afford it?"

"Well, he owns the construction company. It looks like his business is doing well, but he doesn't have any family money."

Kaila looked out the window and watched as the snow fell and lights sparkled against the white. It was beautiful this time of year. The only thing Kaila missed was the daylight; the days were getting shorter. Soon the Christmas season would be upon them and shopping would begin in earnest. Kaila loved shopping for presents and was usually done by the beginning of December. She could then enjoy the rest of the season and not have to be worried and stressed.

Chapter 32

He was getting antsy and looked at his watch for the hundredth time. Finally, it was time.

"Hello." A woman answered the phone.

"Hi, this is Frank. Julie called me and said I could take the kids, she's going to be late tonight."

"She never called me," the woman said, with suspicion in her voice.

"It was a last minute thing. She called me right before she went into the meeting. Can you get the kids ready? I should be right there."

"Alright," she said hesitantly.

He almost blew it, having to choke her name out instead of bitch! He hung up with a grin. It was beginning; nothing was going to stop him now. He pulled back into traffic and sped away.

He slowed to a stop in front of the house and savored his victory. *Never again;* he wouldn't ever again have to take her shit; wouldn't have to see this place. He sauntered up to the door with a spring in his step and rang the bell. He saw the curtain close out of the corner of his eye and the door opened. The bitch's regular lady was on the other side with a frown on her face.

"Hello, Mr. Larson. I haven't gotten ahold of Julie yet. I'm not sure about this."

Before he could answer, his kids ran into the room. "Dad!" they both yelled and rushed past the bulldog and into his arms.

"Do you have your things ready?" he asked.

"Yes!" they chorused.

"Well, go get them," he urged, then with a grin patted their butts as they ran back in.

"I'm still not sure," the lady said.

Frank clenched his fist and took a deep breath. "Aah, don't worry about it. You can try her after the meeting." He tried to smile.

"Fine," she said. "Come in and I'll help the kids."

Frank stood in the doorway, moving from foot to foot. *What's taking them so long?* he thought, checking his watch.

"We're ready," his daughter said as they lugged their bags towards the door.

"Let's go, kids, this is going to be great!"

They cheered as they followed him out to the car. He could see her watching through the window. Damn, his plans had to be altered a bit.

"Hey, kids, you wait here a minute. I just have to talk with the babysitter for a minute."

He locked the doors and headed back.

"What?" she asked.

"Sorry, but Alice forgot her stuffed bunny."

"I swear we packed it. Just wait here."

Frank closed and locked the door quietly, and then followed her to the back.

"What took you so long?" Alice whined.

"Sorry, honey, we were just calling your mother. I'm taking you to a fancy hotel."

"Yeah! Can we order room service?"

"Of course. I just have to go out for a bit, so you guys can watch a movie and order food."

He watched grins split their faces and his heart swelled. They were worth everything.

The kids followed him into the hotel and they stopped at the front for the keys.

"OK, kids. Here are the rules. You do not leave this room. You don't call anyone or let anyone in and we'll order you food before I go, and you can pick a movie."

The kids dropped their bags and jumped on the bed, grabbing the remote. There was a brief power struggle before Alice held up the remote in triumph.

"Quick, kids, we need to order, I have to get going."

Frank drummed his fingers on the steering wheel. *Where the heck was she?* The meeting had been over for ten minutes already. Just then Julie walked out alone, playing with her phone and headed for her car.

"Crap!" He hoped she didn't get the message from the babysitter. "Julie, just a sec."

Julie glanced over in surprise and stopped. "What are you doing here?" she demanded nervously.

"I need to talk to you about the kids. Can you please come? It'll only take a few minutes." Frank had a hard time saying the words and keeping the smile on his face.

Julie approached him warily and opened the car door.

"Get in, it'll be warmer." Frank watched as she sealed her doom.

"The police stopped by the house asking about you."

"What! Did they say why?"

"No. They just had some questions."

"Maybe it was about the kids from the club that were killed."

"So, what did you want to talk about?"

"This has to stop, what's happening between us," Frank said, waving his arms.

Julie looked relieved as she said, "Finally. We need to work it out for the kids. They're getting hurt."

"Oh, we will," Frank said with an evil smile and put the car into gear.

"What are you doing?" Julie demanded in alarm and turned towards the door, trying to open it, but realized the handle was missing. Before she could scream, Frank reached over and hit her across the head.

Thank God, she's quiet now. Frank swerved out of the parking lot and headed to the cabin.

Chapter 33

"What's with the lights always being out?" George asked. "Let's go check it out."

They climbed out of the truck and walked to the door. While George rang the bell, Kaila stepped up to the window and peered in.

"Hey, George, there's a light on in the back.... Is that a leg?" Kaila said in alarm.

George scooted over and looked in. "Come on," he said and rammed the front door. After a couple of rushes, the doorframe splintered and they ran towards the light.

"Oh my god, who is it?" Kaila whispered.

"I'm not sure."

They stared at the body of an older woman whose body was bent at a weird angle.

George pulled out his phone to call the station.

"Where are the kids? Where's Mrs. Larson?" Kaila asked. "Maybe this wouldn't have happened if we came earlier."

"Don't start thinking that, you couldn't have known," George said as they hurried through the house looking for any signs of life.

"We need to find him. I'm sure it's him," Kaila said.

"Let's see if we can find out if there's any other properties under Frank's name," George said.

Once the officers arrived, they headed back to the station and got to work.

"George, I think I found something. He just bought a cabin out of town four months ago. Guess what else? He owns a mustang. Isn't that the vehicle you thought was possibly used in the kidnapping?"

"Yeah. It's starting to look like Mr. Larson is our guy. But what's he doing with his family?"

"We need to get to his cabin now!" Kaila said, grabbing her things, a bad feeling in the pit of her stomach.

Chapter 34

Frank slapped the bitch's face. "Wake up," he snarled.

Julie slowly opened her eyes and a look of horror crossed her face as she tried to move. Ropes were wrapped around her body and legs, keeping her tied to a table. She could glimpse garbage bags lying on the floor. Shivers ran down her spine as she imagined why they were there.

"What's going on?" she croaked out, trying to shift free.

"Don't bother trying, you're not getting away," he said gleefully as he picked up his knives.

"You can't do this! Why?" she cried.

"Because you're keeping me away from my kids. You don't deserve to live."

"You don't deserve them," she yelled. Frank wound up and hit her in the face. Blood dripped from her lips and onto the table. He clapped excitedly and turned around to his knives.

"Where are they?"

"Don't worry yourself about them. They're safe and you won't be seeing them again."

She started to cry. "Please don't do this. I don't want to die."

"Well, you should have thought about that before trying to take them away from me."

"What did you do with Mrs. Robinson?"

"I had to get rid of her."

"Oh no!" More tears fell and soaked beneath her head.

"Now, I wanted this to last a while, but there's not enough time now, they're waiting."

As they were talking, Frank didn't notice the police surrounding the cabin.

Kaila and George slowly stalked up the steps, guns drawn. George signaled for Kaila to stop and quietly jiggled the handle and nodded. Kaila braced herself with a grimace as George flung open the door and jumped into the room, with Kaila behind him.

"Freeze, Mr. Larson! Police!"

Frank swung to face them with the knife held high.

"Frank, put down the knife, you're surrounded," Kaila yelled. She glimpsed Julie behind him tied to a table. Her face was red; Kaila could see a bruise forming on one of her eyes.

Frank glanced indecisively back at the bitch, trying to decide if it would be worth it. *Maybe if I'm quick, one good stab would do it,* he thought.

"Don't do it, Frank," George warned and cocked his gun; the sound echoed in the room. More officers ran in from the rear of the cabin and Frank cried out in despair, dropping the knife. George surged forward and threw Frank to the ground, cuffing him.

Kaila ran to the table and started working on the knots.

"It's alright, Julie, you're safe, don't worry." Kaila helped her sit up and held her steady when Julie swayed.

"Do you know where my babies are?" she sobbed.

"We're hoping you knew."

"He wouldn't tell me."

"Frank, where are your kids?" Kaila demanded, turning towards him.

Frank sneered at her. "I'm not telling you. They're safe and she's not getting them."

"You can't do this!" Julie screeched, straining against Kaila, her claws reaching.

"Don't worry, we'll find them," Kaila said as Julie escaped and tried attacking Frank. Kaila spun and grabbed her around the waist, pulling her back.

"Julie, you can't!" George yanked a grinning Frank out the door and to the waiting squad car.

"Detective, please take Mrs. Larson to the ER and get her checked out," Kaila asked, leading Julie to the door.

"I don't want to go. I need to find my children."

"That's our job, we'll let you know. Before you go, can you tell me if Frank had any family or close friends in town?"

"No. He has a few relatives in British Colombia."

"Thanks. Please, go with the detective and get checked out. We will contact you," Kaila urged softly.

As the officers walked by, Kaila whispered,

"Make sure you keep an eye on her, don't leave."

"No problem."

"Let's examine the cabin and see if we can find any clues on the whereabouts of his kids," George said, coming back in.

Kaila put on her gloves and started her search in the main room. She strode towards the corner where the only shelves in the room stood. There were three shelves. The first one had a picture with Frank and two grinning children. The second was empty -- but the last -- "Oh my god. Trophies!"

"What did you find?" George called out.

"I recognize these, they're Victoria's glasses, and I'm sure these other two items will be Gerald's and Rachel's." Kaila picked up the crushed phone and ring and nodded to an officer who brought over a bag and she dropped them in.

"We need to check; I'm sure there's going to be blood here. This is probably were he killed them," Kaila said.

"Yes. Let's head back to the station. We need to get Frank to talk," George agreed.

They rushed out, leaving the rest of the officers there to finish.

"Where're you keeping him?" George asked as they stomped into the station.

"He's in Interview 1," the officer at the desk replied.

When they reached the room and peered through the glass, Frank was rocking back and forth, singing, "Hush little baby, don't say a word, Papa's gonna buy you a mockingbird. If that mockingbird don't sing, Papa's gonna buy you a diamond ring...."

"What are you doing here?" Kaila demanded as she glared at the detective guarding Julie.

"I'm fine," she said and turned back to watch her ex.

"What's he singing?" George asked.

"It's the song that he sang to the kids every night," Julie said softly.

"How long has he been doing this?" Kaila asked.

"Since they brought him in," the detective answered.

262

Kaila moved closer to the window and watched Frank. His eyes were glazed over and his arms were wrapped around his body as he rocked.

"Well, let's try this," George said with a sigh and entered the room with Kaila close behind.

"Hello, Frank," George said.

Frank glanced up at them, but continued rocking.

At least that eerie singing stopped, Kaila thought. "Frank, where did you take your kids? We need to make sure they're all right," Kaila asked.

Frank turned to stare at her. "They're fine." And he started to sing again, causing shivers to run up Kaila's back.

"Frank, how can you be sure? What if they're hungry or cold? They are still alive, right?" Kaila demanded.

"I would never harm my kids," Frank screeched.

"What about those three other kids you murdered?" George asked.

"They deserved it. I was told it had to be done."

George looked over in surprise at Kaila. "Who told you?" he asked.

"I had to say! I'm sorry," Frank cried out as he stared at something above him.

"Who's they?" Kaila questioned, bringing his focus back to her.

"The voices, they told me it was necessary."

"Why?"

"Because they're horrible!"

"You're saying these kids deserved this?"

"I'm not talking!" Frank started rocking.

"I wonder if he took them to a hotel," Kaila said. "We need to start calling."

"No!" Frank screeched. "She can't have them." Kaila watched as tears coursed down his cheeks and his rocking became frantic. Kaila and George dashed out of the room.

"I want to help," Julie demanded.

"Julie, you need to stay here and let us do our job. OK," Kaila said, putting a hand on her arm.

They organized everyone into areas and started calling hotels and motels.

An hour later, Kaila gave a triumphant yell. "I've got them. They're at the Sheraton in the north end."

"Let's get going," George said.

"I'm coming," yelled Julie.

"Fine, but you stay back with the officers," George answered.

Because it was late, the drive to the hotel was relatively quick.

"Hello, I called earlier. I need to know what room Frank Larson rented," Kaila demanded, flashing her badge.

The clerk peered at the crowd in front of her before typing into the computer. "Room 306."

"We need the key," Kaila said and held out her hand.

"OK, Julie, you're waiting out here until we see what's inside," George said as they stood outside room 306.

"You mean they may not be alive?" she said with anguish.

Kaila knocked on the door and said, "Police." She waited a few minutes and tried again.

"How do we know you're the police?" a little voice demanded.

A smile split Kaila's face as she said, "Good question, honey. Are you able to see through the keyhole? I'm holding my badge up." They could hear scraping as the kids must have been dragging a chair to the door.

A minute later the lock clicked and the door slowly opened.

"See, I'm from the police department and this is my partner." George smiled at the two sleepy faces peering up at them.

"We've been looking for you," Kaila said. "Are you alright?"

"Yes, Daddy let us order room service and he said we're going on a trip. Where's Daddy?" the little girl asked.

"Well, he couldn't come, but we brought your mom." Kaila nodded and the officer let Julie go so she could run up to the kids with open arms.

"I'm so glad you're alright," Julie whispered, holding back tears. The children hugged her back.

"We were fine, Mom. What happened to your face?" Alice asked.

Julie put her hand up to her eye. "I slipped on some ice."

"Julie, how about we get you another room here. You shouldn't go back to your house yet," Kaila said softly. Julie looked up and nodded her head in agreement. Kaila left the room to make the arrangements.

Chapter 35

"I'm exhausted," Kaila said, collapsing in her chair.

"Let's go home. We'll leave him stewing till morning. We've stopped the killer," George said.

"If I can make it home," Kaila joked, feeling the adrenaline leaving her body. "See you in the morning."

Kaila let herself into the apartment, dropping her things by the door. She fell into the kitchen chair and unwrapped her sub, digging in. Echo was barking in the back and Kaila scarfed the rest of her dinner down before going to let him out.

"I know, Echo, I'm so sorry. But I caught a bad man tonight," Kaila said, snuggling up to him as he tried to wiggle away. She let go of his squirming form and laughed as he jumped and twisted away towards the door.

"I'm so tired, but we'll go quick once around the block," Kaila said, grabbing his leash.

Kaila reached for the door, but it opened and she pitched forward slightly.

"Sorry, Kaila." Holly laughed and helped Kaila right herself.

"It's fine. Do you want to come for a quick trip around the block?"

"Sure, why not. Give me a sec."

"We caught him!" Kaila said excitedly as they left the building.

"That's great! Who was he?"

"We're not sure of the motive yet, but we caught him trying to kill his ex-wife."

"Really. Is she alright?"

"Yes, and we found where he stashed his kids."

"That's good. What's next?"

"Rest tonight and tomorrow we get some answers," Kaila answered as they came up to their building.

"So, are you ready?" Kaila asked, walking up to George.

"Yep. Let's go talk to this kook."

"Was he watched last night?"

"We had him on suicide watch. He didn't try anything."

"Is he still unstable?"

"He seems a little better. We'll see when we start questioning him. Let's go."

They stepped into the room and considered Frank behind the table. His eyes were bloodshot, his hair matted and he had lots of beard stubble, but he wasn't rocking and singing anymore.

They both sat across from him and George pulled out the pictures of the three dead teens.

"Frank, do you want to tell me about them?" George asked, tapping the pictures.

Frank gave them a cursory glance before saying, "Why should I help you?"

"Don't you want to tell your story, make us understand why they deserved it? Isn't that what you told us yesterday?" Kaila asked.

"I didn't say that," Frank muttered, twisting his body.

"Yes, you did. Last night you said the kids deserved it. The voices told you to do it."

Frank looked unsure as he said, "I didn't tell you that; I wouldn't." He shook his head in denial.

"You wanted us to know, Frank, that must be why you said something."

Frank seemed to fold into himself and he covered his face and mumbled, "They told me I had to. It was necessary. But they lied."

"Who told you?"

"They did!" Frank started to get agitated and punched his head a couple of times.

"Hey, hey. Calm down, it's alright," Kaila said softly.

"What did they lie about?"

"That everything was going to be OK. That I would have my kids." Frank looked over. "It's all her fault, you know."

"Whose?" George asked.

"The bitch's." he snarled.

"You mean Julie?" Kaila inquired.

"She blamed me for losing the money. It's not my fault!" he yelled, stabbing at his chest.

"Why did you lose your money? Were you gambling?" George asked.

"Of course not. It wasn't my fault! They said it was a guarantee."

"What happened?" Kaila coaxed.

"It's their fault; they did it."

"Who did, was it someone from the club?"

Frank closed off and just stared at them, his foot tapping on the floor.

269

"Come on, Frank, do you really want to let them get away with it? You're going away for a long time, do you want to be the only one?"

"You won't do anything, they're rich. Their fancy lawyers will get them off with a slap on the wrist." He snorted.

"Yes, we will. If they've done something criminal, they will answer for it," Kaila promised.

Frank looked at her with skepticism. "Fine. It's all of them. Vance, John and Tyson.

"What did they do?"

"They took my money, that's what they did!"

"How did they do it?"

"It was supposed to be for some investment. They said it went under and wouldn't give me my money back. So, the bitch left me and took my kids with her. How are they? I want to see them!" Frank demanded.

Kaila and George shared a glance before she said, "Sorry, but that's not possible. You're in a lot of trouble." She stood up and stepped out of the room, motioning for an officer.

"Take him back to his cell." Kaila motioned to Frank.

"I want to see a lawyer," Frank yelled from the room.

"You can make a call," Kaila said.

"I bet that's what the employee from the club was talking about. I wonder if there're any other disgruntled investors," Kaila said to George as they headed back to the desks.

"Well, I guess we should go see the fraud unit and get them to investigate these three," George said with a sigh.

"Let's hurry. I know their kids' death is probably a horrible consequence, but they should be charged," Kaila said. They grabbed everything they had on the victims' parents and headed over to the other department.

"Hi, guys," Kaila said, walking in.

"Hi. What can we do for you?"

"We might have a case for you. We've arrested a serial killer and he's said it was revenge against the victim's parents for stealing his money. He snapped."

The detective held out his hands for the files and began flipping through them.

"You say that your suspect is blaming these men?"

"Yes, they all went to the same club, but Frank joined just over a year ago."

"Fresh meat. Do you know if they dealt with anyone else at the club?"

"We never investigated that, we just found out. There are a couple of detectives at the club questioning everyone and they may have found something more."

"Can you send them our way then with their information and we'll check into it."

"Can you let us know what the results of your investigation are? I'm sure the prosecution and Mr. Larson's lawyer will be interested as well."

"No problem. We'll contact you if we have any questions."

"Thanks," Kaila said.

"Should we call the families and let them know we got him?"

"We'll first meet with the other teams and brief them on what's happened. We'll want to watch what we tell the parents so we don't alert them to the other investigation until the detectives want them aware."

"I'll get everyone together," Kaila said, heading off.

After their briefing and phone calls to the parents, Kaila was moving files around her desk.

"I'm so glad we can close this case," George said with a sigh.

"I just wish we could have stopped him sooner."

"Don't go there. You can't change things and you'll make yourself crazy thinking that way," George warned.

"Yeah, I know," Kaila answered. "Do you think those men were involved?"

"I can see it, but can you imagine how they'll feel if it's because of them their kids were killed?"

"That would be heartbreaking," Kaila agreed. "Hopefully the fraud unit finds something quickly and lets us know."

The next couple of weeks passed quietly for Kaila. She was able to catch up on sleep and had time to visit with friends. They worked diligently on their open cases and were even able to close a couple more. Kaila was sitting at her desk typing when her phone rang.

"Hello," she said.

"Hi, this is Detective Zee, from the fraud unit. I thought you'd like to know we're bringing them in."

"Really. Thanks, can we come down?"

"Sure."

Kaila hung up and turned to George. "They're being brought in. Do you want to go?"

"Hell yes. I want to hear their excuses."

They both hurried down to the other department and were just in time to see the three men coming through the door in handcuffs, with their wives in tow. Vance looked up, saw them, and yelled, "This is your doing! After everything our family has been through—"

"Sorry, but we weren't the ones stealing other peoples' money," George commented.

Vance sneered as they were led to separate interview rooms. Their wives were held back from entering and the doors shut.

Mrs. Radcliff turned to Kaila and asked with tears in her eyes, "Was this the reason my baby was killed?"

"It may have been. I'm sorry."

She sat down in the chair and put her face in her hands. Kaila and George watched the interrogations and just shook their heads. Vance was a hard nut to crack; he refused to answer any questions and demanded to see his lawyer. However, the other two folded like a deck of cards. They had been running a Ponzi scheme and had promised higher than usual returns to their investors, but so far it was only Frank that they had told the investment had collapsed. Usually people that ran this scheme skipped town after; they had been trying to bleed everyone dry first. There were only a few other members of the club that they had scammed, because they were trying to stay away from their watering hole. When Frank had showed up, and was so gullible, they couldn't resist. Kaila had to look away when it was revealed that Frank was the killer; to see the look of horror crossing their faces was hard to bear. That was Vance's breaking point; at least Kaila finally saw that he loved his daughter. When they were led out of the rooms, Mrs. Radcliff stared at her husband in horror and screamed, "It's all your fault! How could you kill our son?" And she dove at him, but was grabbed by one of the detectives.

Kaila and George left the room. "That was horrible. Do you think Frank will have a defense?"

"No, even if they bankrupted him, a jury won't excuse his behavior."

"I know greed is a powerful motivator, but these families already had excessive amounts of money. Why risk it all? Usually with this scheme the family would need to move. These men were willing to leave it all?"

"Probably for the thrill."

Kaila shook her head. "I wonder if Frank's going to try and plead insanity or something similar."

"I haven't heard. Come on, let's go grab a drink and celebrate."

"That's the best idea I've heard in a long time." Kaila said, smiling.

THE END

If you have finished reading SWEETEST REVENGE, an honest review on Amazon and Goodreads would be very much appreciated.

Thank you very much—

Yvonne Yourkowski

FREE PREVIEW
OF YVONNE YOURKOWSKI'S NEXT RELEASE

CHAPTER 1

"I want more money!" the man demanded over the phone as he flailed his arms in agitation. "You killed that man and I should be going to the police."

There was silence on the other end before a low growl came through the line. "Don't threaten me, you won't like the outcome."

The man felt a shudder travel through his body and he almost caved in. "Half a million deposited in the same account—or you'll be sorry," he said, and then slammed the phone down. Feeling giddy as the adrenalin left his large body, he collapsed in the awaiting chair. Tonight would be soon enough to check his account, and then maybe a trip out of town would be a good idea. Smiling with anticipation, he headed to the kitchen looking for food.

"Hurry up, Peter!" Duncan yelled, while he splashed gasoline on the large wooden kitchen table and matching chairs.

"I'm coming," Peter hollered back from somewhere within the house.

Duncan glanced around and grimaced in disgust. The room was sparsely furnished other than the table and chairs, which were soaked in gas. Probably all he could fit in, he thought snidely.

The walls were a cheery yellow, and the white cabinets seemed to shine. He finished coating the kitchen and moved onto the living room. Maybe just a bit to ensure the flames continued their path of destruction, Duncan thought. Where in the hell was Peter? He only had one job. Just than the figure of his ire ambled in casually, like he was on vacation.

"Where the hell were you?" Duncan demanded.

"Just having a little bit of fun." Peter grinned.

"Where's the body?"

"I left him in the bedroom."

"Well, bring him in the living room, we want to make sure he burns."

"Fine, fine," Peter grumbled. "Come and help, he must weigh a ton."

"Gimme me a minute to finish this. Did you make sure all the doors were secure?"

"Yes. Hurry up! I want to escape before we're spotted."

"Now you're in a rush." Duncan dropped the container and followed Peter to the bedroom in the back of the house. When they entered Duncan spotted the large body collapsed on the floor and frowned.

"You grab his arms and I'll take the legs," Duncan commanded.

"How come you get the easier part?"

"Because I would have drugged him in the living room so we didn't have to carry the body, you great blithering moron."

Peter grimaced before heaving the man beneath his armpits and groaned. "We're doing this guy a favour," Peter said as they lugged him towards his impending doom.

"You made sure of the correct dosage, right?" Duncan questioned as he let Peter almost drag the body down the dark hallway. He smelled the gasoline and could already start feeling the smoke burn his eyes as the furniture began dancing in flames.

"I'm not an idiot. I took into account all his fat."

"Good. We don't want him trying to escape, but at least the doors are barred. What about the injection site, was it between the toes?" Duncan asked, looking at Peter for confirmation.

"Quit questioning me, it's not my first rodeo. I already said I did," Peter snarled.

Duncan kept quiet as they dropped the body and rolled him over on his stomach by the couch. Usually Peter was easygoing, but when he became angry, you'd better watch out. That guy had an explosive temper and let his fists do the talking. The last guy who worked for the boss ended up on the wrong side of Peter and ate through a straw for quite a while. Duncan peeked through the thin striped curtains and cursed the full moon shining through. Hopefully no one saw their escape. He looked back and saw Peter giving a couple of kicks to the prone body, a grin playing on his lips. Duncan sighed before motioning him to follow to the back door, bending down for the jerry can still half filled with fuel on his way.

"Do you have the matches?" Peter asked.

"Yeah, they're in here," Duncan answered, fumbling in his pocket.

They stepped up to the kitchen doorway. Duncan swiped the match and stared at the flickering flame a minute before throwing it towards the table. They gazed at the rising flames as if in a trance for a minute. Duncan shook his head before rushing out, with Peter close behind. They jammed the nail at the top of the door as they left and then booted across the yard into the back alley. Smoke and flames were just becoming noticeable from their position.

"That's a beautiful sight," Peter said with a sigh as he paused again to watch.

"Come on, we can watch from a safer distance," Duncan whispered, dragging Peter along.

Keeping low and to the shadows, they ran the couple of blocks to their waiting car. Once safely inside, they both grinned and laughed with excitement. The whole escape had taken less than five minutes, but Duncan could already hear the sirens. Damn, hopefully they wouldn't make it in time to save the bastard, he thought. Neighbours were scattered along the street staring in wonder at the burning house. The men stopped a block away, idling as they watched their handiwork.

     The first engine truck squealed to a stop and Officer Norman Fast jumped out, yelling the task assignments as the second truck appeared. They needed search and rescue fighters entering immediately while the fire attack sector tried containing the flames before all the surrounding houses caught on fire.

     "We have a Type 5, wood-frame construction house fully involved, sending two men in," Norman told dispatch as the other engine officer ran up with a pad and pen, writing furiously.

     Norman watched as the men from the second engine ran to the closest hydrant with their hose streaming behind. The senior hose man and his second headed to the front door. They only had minutes before the fire grew too large to contain. A shiver crawled up Norman's spine despite the heat emanating towards him. For some reason, he knew a surprise would be waiting for them, he just didn't know what. His anxiety increased as it became apparent the door wasn't going to cooperate. The fire fighters had to use their forcible-entry tools, and once they broke through, the two men seized the hose and cautiously entered.

     Before Norman did a quick three hundred and sixty degree assessment around the house looking for any exits or good ventilation points, he called in a second alarm to dispatch. The bright yellow and orange flames were already rolling, and at the back of the house, flames were licking out the door, meeting the awaiting winds ready to carry them towards the neighbours. Something was wrong with the door, but

Norman couldn't get close enough to inspect what was secured to the top. It looked like an extra board held the door closed, but he couldn't make a confirmation. Hopefully it wasn't burned away; it was looking like the fire was no accident.

The ladder crew had arrived and were pulling out the fans as Norman rounded the corner. Two other engines and the ambulance crowded the narrow streets in front, blocking the view from all the curious onlookers. But there was one nervous older looking man with a tiny dog standing off to the side of his engine truck. Must be the witness who called in, Norman thought. Dispatch probably told him to wait there for someone to question him. Before approaching him, Norman ensured that the other fire attack crews were creating a water curtain to stop the fire from spreading. Static crackled a moment before a voice came through, "We have a body in the living room." Norman's stomach plummeted as he glanced at the time. The hose stopped moving and seconds later the two firemen struggled through the doorway with a large body. Thick, inky smoke followed the men out, filling the entrance. Paramedics rushed forward to help the fire fighters and the ladder crew gathered up the fans.

"All crews out and try ventilation! Immediate building flashover. Sit until we mitigate the situation before anyone else enters. Chance of survivability is zero," Norman yelled over the noise as the fans were set in front of the door. He watched as the black smoke crawled up the house and caught on fire, joining the other flames trying to escape. Even with their bunker gear on, the fire fighters would only survive for five seconds during a flashover, if there was anyone else inside, they had no chance. They needed to contain the fire now and hope they could preserve this property and the adjoining ones.

Norman stopped beside the thin, shaking witness and asked, "Sir, were you the one who called in the fire?"

"Yes," he squeaked.

"Do you know the residents?"

"Not well. I live a few houses down," he said, pointing down the street.

"How many people lived here?"

"Only Barnaby. I've never seen anyone else. He may have visitors, but not for long."

Norman felt a small spark of hope that no other bodies were being left to burn inside.

Duncan and Peter left the safety of their car and slowly inched closer to the burning house.

"This is close enough," Duncan whispered.

"We need to get closer to see."

"Someone might realize we're not from around here and say something."

"Not likely." Peter snorted. "People driving by stop all the time. Stop worrying. I want to make sure the deed is done."

Just then they watched as two fire fighters carried out the body.

"Crap!" Peter snarled. "What are we going to tell the boss?"

"Don't worry. If you gave the right dosage, even if he woke up, I'm sure the smoke got him. Even from here, he looks a little black. No way he's talking."

"Fine. Let's get out of here, you get to do the explaining."

It felt like hours before Norman could say the fire was under control and allow the three crews back into the house. The primary search still had to be completed and they needed to ensure the fire was out and didn't rekindle. A couple years back in another city, the fire department declared a fire was out earlier on and the owner was then allowed back onto the property, but the fire rekindled and he was killed. Of course, the fire department was blamed for not doing their job, even though they didn't have the authority anymore to stop the owner from entering. That's why they now usually waited several days before saying the fire was out, ensuring no rekindling and that they were still in charge of the scene.

Norman now had time to secure the scene and call in the police. The paramedics weren't able to save Barnaby; it was looking like a successful murder.

Made in the USA
Columbia, SC
19 November 2019